Elin's Air

EMILY STANFORD

Hillman Publishing

First published in Great Britain by Hillman Publishing, 2016

Hillman Publishing
Email: books@hillmanpublishing.co.uk
Web: www.hillmanpublishing.com

ISBN 978-1-909996-11-3

A Catalogue record for this book is available from the British Library

Typeset by Hillman Publishing
Cover painting by Morgan Hebner
Cover design by Hillman Publishing

Printed and bound in Great Britain by
Lightning Source UK Ltd, Milton Keynes, Bucks

Hillman Publishing is an imprint of Coastal Peak Ltd

Acknowledgements

"Alone we can do so little; together we can do so much." —*Helen Keller*

My name might be what everyone reads on the front cover, but in truth, Elin's Air is a patchwork of encouragement, patience, skill and input from others, that I have sewn together into words on a page. I have mountains of gratitude for all those who have contributed to this creation in some way.

My thanks to: Hillman Publishing for being willing to take a risk with me and making my dream a reality; Emily—the 'editor midwife', patient and wise, in helping me deliver; Seymour for cleaning up and tidying my grammatical messes with a 'no nonsense' approach; Morgan for drawing the cover as I described Elin to her, and then filling in the backdrop with incredible skill and ease; Manon for correcting the Welsh and ensuring it was in the right vernacular; Annette for encouraging me to 'keep writing' after reading the first portion; all those who read a draft and made constructive comments, or answered my random queries on 'how to say' or 'is this correct?'— Cate, Suzanne, Freya, Christine, Jess, Sarah, Siân, Becky, Simeon, Jayne, and Jessica; my mother-in-law, Ruth, who painstakingly proofread, while feeling poorly; my children for enduring me staring at my laptop for hours and telling them not to disturb me; my husband, Tim, for encouraging me to write; my King, Jesus, for the gift of being able to serve Him.

Dedicated to

Josiah, Simeon, Ruth and Jemimah

Book One

Chapter One

The lighthouse on *Ynys Môn* flashed on, off, twinkling in the distance and the evening star shone bright and constant above it. I could almost see Ireland. The sky went from a deep gold by the water's edge, through a lighter yellow to pastel green and blue. Pink clouds broke up the blue. The closer they came to me the redder they got. A red sky at night—that foretold a good story for tomorrow. Either that, or the shepherd's socks were on fire. I chuckled to myself as I remembered William cracking that joke the night we went ferreting in the rabbit warrens at the edge of the woods.

I had held the nets while William put his ferrets down to flush out the rabbits. We caught a few, and William was quick to wring their necks. It sickened me, but it was all over in a second. Then they were in his bag and ready to go to his mother to skin and gut. Sure enough, the day that followed was glorious.

It was chilly now the sun had gone. I nestled against the stone and heather, to keep out of the wind, and looked down at the quarry. In the dusk it stood out like a giant's staircase cut into the mountainside. Dad and Ifan chipped away at that staircase day in, day out for pay that seemed to wane at the manager's whim. Camaraderie and loyalty ran thicker than blood amongst the quarrymen in the *caban*, but these were lean days, where unions and strikes shaved income thin. The words the men used meant little to me, but I knew from their talk that there was less to live off than there used to be, and the men always sounded grieved and angry.

I had left Mam visiting Bethan's grave. She was the only one of Mam's children who had a stone in the cemetery; it had been bought with money Nain gave Mam. The rest of the children were remembered by the mounds they left. Bethan's little slate headstone had begun to tilt towards the sea. Beside her lay Tobias and Sioned, who died days old.

Mam had battled many weaknesses and sickness in her babies. Even Llinos, the eldest, who now lived on the cliffs towards Caernarfon, was weak. But Mam said when Dewi was born he was strong and their fortunes changed. The new terraces in the village were built from sturdy quarry stone and did a good job of keeping the wind and rain out. Unfortunately, it was not enough to protect Manon, who never saw her fifth year, nor Guto the same, but the twins, Ifan and Ceinwen, thrived.

Five lost babies lay buried side by side in the *mynwent*, each with a piece of Mam's heart. Their names were in the Bible above the range and she never forgot their birthdays as they passed year by year. But it was only on Bethan's birthday—today—that she would come and sit at the foot of Bethan's stone. As the youngest, I never knew those deceased brothers and sisters and couldn't share Mam's grief.

I had found an outcrop where I could sit and look out, imagining kingdoms beyond my eye's reach. When the sun had gone, I stood and ruffled the clinging bits of heather from my skirts.

Away, through the heather I heard a shout, like a call for help. Startled, I jumped. I listened. A scream pierced me. It was close. My heart thumped loudly in my ears. I held my breath as the sound came again. It was a squeal, but this time I knew it was not a human cry.

I moved towards the silhouette of the mountains, nearer the sound. All was silent. My skirt hushed against the heather and I held my breath in case I should hear the cry again.

There was nothing. Then suddenly I saw it. Like a fish out of water, a rabbit was flapping and floundering on the edge of the path the quarrymen had worn, springing and recoiling. Just for a minute it lay still, hauling breath into its lungs, its sides rapidly rising and sinking into a hollow pit beneath the ribs. Then it began vigorously twisting and pulling in vain. I could see the cruel wire biting tighter.

"Don't struggle, little one."

I grabbed its writhing body and could see the whites of its eyes. Slipping my finger beneath the snare, I loosened it from the rabbit's neck. It panted in shock until it had gained enough strength to hop unsteadily into the heather. Pulling the loop of the snare straight so that nothing else would get caught, I turned on my heel and went back down the hill.

As I approached the cemetery wall, I could see a man standing talking to Mam. His face was under the shadow of his hat. I came close and he looked up. It was Mr Price, Gweinidog, the Methodist minister from the village. He had studied at Oxford. I still wondered why God had brought him to our village. He did not seem to fit in well. He was tall, with English ways and his sermons rambled on with lots of words I never followed. This did not deter us from going every week to listen to him. Some weeks he was dramatic and used a special voice to illustrate his ramblings. I tried not to catch the eyes of my friends on those occasions. Our giggles were hard to keep under cloak and adults would hiss at us to be quiet. But sometimes it was too funny. I wanted to share the joke and would look for William. He was not always there.

I think Mr Price meant well, but any kindness was given out of a sense of duty. Mam's goodbye to him was short and curt. He touched his hat and walked up the path I had just come down.

In the failing light, I noticed some sacking in his hand. The snare…! It was his? I would have thought the minister was well enough off not to need extra meat, but life was full of inconsistencies. I had just freed a rabbit from a snare and yet, I was happy to go ferreting with William and watch him kill and bag other rabbits.

Mam caught at my hand impatiently and chivvied me on. The wind was picking up.

"Come on, Elin."

She had something on her mind.

Chapter Two

"Mam," I called as I opened the door. I put my basket down and spoke again without looking up. "Can I go and see the lambs at Nant Uchaf? William asked me."

I waited. There was no answer.

"Mam?" I shouted up the stairs.

No reply. Fresh coal covered the flames in the grate. On the table in the back room there were two loaves of bread sitting on trivets. It was Mam's day to use the community oven. As I rested my hand against the crust to absorb the warmth, I noticed the outhouse door was open. I went through and there was Mam with a muddy leek hanging down against her apron. Her eyes were fixed on Mrs Jones, who was doing all the talking. They stood either side of the low, slate wall that divided the gardens. Mrs Jones smiled as I skirted the vegetable beds.

"You never can tell though, Annie. You never can tell." Her slow, melodic words danced across to me and Mam turned.

"Ah! Elin! There's a loaf of bread on the table. Can you take it to Mrs Roberts, please? She had her baby this morning—another boy." Mam and Mrs Jones shook their heads together, their tongues clicking mechanically.

"Let's hope this one is a keeper," Mrs Jones said in an undertone, leaning close to Mam's ear. A cloud of sadness passed over her face, "Not like the last."

"Yes, Mam." I answered. "Can I go and see the lambs at Nant Uchaf? William says there are lots."

She said I could and to get some more butter from Mrs Gruffudd while I was there.

"Put your coat on, cariad. The wind has picked up."

"*Diolch, Mam. Dwi'n mynd.*" I called, jumping over the edge of the vegetable bed.

"Don't forget to come home as soon as the sun disappears behind the mountain, Elin." Mam called after me.

As if I'd forget? "*Turn for home when the sun slips behind the mountain.*" Guidance whispered from parent to child, generation to generation. I could not remember a day when that rule had not governed my freedom. We lived in the shadow of the mountain and our valley darkened at least an hour before the sun actually set. I delivered the bread, comfortably warm under my coat, to Mrs Roberts and her new baby at number twelve and then set off up the hill and out of the village.

Nant Uchaf was one of three farms in the valley and sat high above the rest, looking out to sea. It was a steep climb, but my stout and sturdy legs were well used to it. The farm was once the summer pasture for Nant Isaf. Since the quarry had grown and more men needed feeding, it was farmed all year round, by Uncle John. He had been married to Mam's sister, Dilys, who died when Owen was born. Years later, Uncle John married a lady from Trem y Mynydd. Jane was a spinster who was older than him and an excellent cook.

"Hello Elin!" Uncle John's hearty voice hailed me.

"What brings you up here?" He grinned from the other side of a wooden gate. Meg began barking excitedly when she saw me. Unable to help herself, she jumped the gate with a flying leap and ran to greet me. I laughed and bent down to stroke her. There was only one Meg. With her tail guiding her, a rudder constantly moving, she twisted and turned rapidly, wrapping herself round my arm as I stroked her, first this way then the other.

"Oh Meg," I said, rising to greet Uncle John. "Mam wants some more butter and I've come to see the lambs. William says you have lots."

"We have. There were some twins born this morning but their Mam didn't make it. They're in the kitchen. Go and see them, if you like, and Jane will give you your butter. William was in the shippon when I last saw him. He can take you up the hill to see the others when he's done. Tell him I said so."

"*Diolch!*" I liked Uncle John. He was always steady and calm and kind; even when Aunt Dilys had died it seemed as if he kept his course and continued in his quiet way, looking after Owen on his own until he met Jane. The only change was that after Dilys had died, he had started going to the Presbyterian chapel up in Trem y Mynydd instead of the Methodist one down in Nant.

I ran, while Meg barked at me, all the way up to the motley collection of whitewashed, stone buildings that nestled into the slope. Just before I reached them, I saw the door was open into the walled orchard, and I could not resist. I snuck in. Daffodils carpeted the grass and made it bright. This little orchard was always just right: warm when everywhere else felt cold, or full of shade when everywhere else felt hot; quiet when everywhere else was a bustle, and welcoming when everywhere else was lonely. It was my favourite place on the farm and I had first come here when I was small because some of the fruit trees were the perfect size to climb. I swung my leg onto the old apple tree by the wall. It was effortless now. Leaning against the trunk, I looked at the cherry trees and wondered how easily I could climb them now I was taller.

It had to be done. I got down, avoided treading on daffodils and jumped to catch the lower branch of the cherry tree nearest to me. I hung upside down with my ankles locked in a cross. My skirts went everywhere. In a second, I swung myself around the branch and was upright, sitting as if on a horse.

I could see above the walls out to sea. What a view! I giggled. I was big enough to climb the cherry trees.

"Well now, Elin," my cousin Owen called to me from the orchard door. He was shading his eyes and squinting at me.

"You're getting a bit big to be tree climbing."

I laughed back at him.

"Look! I've done it. I never climbed a cherry tree before."

"Now you're big enough for that, your Mam will soon be putting you out to work," he joked. "Come and pick the cherries in the summer. We'll send you up the ladders." He waved and was gone.

I slipped down. Uncle John had said William would be in the shippon, and Mam wanted butter. I headed for the kitchen.

Chapter Three

The kitchen door was open and sunlight spilled across
the flags. I pushed it wider until the sunlight reached in to
embrace the enormous fireplace, illuminating a roughly
hewn wooden box beside the fire.

"*Helo!*" I called, expecting an answer from the pantry.
I couldn't see anybody in the shadows. The answer I got
was a feeble bleat from by the fire. In an instant, I was on
my knees beside the box, caressing the bony heads of two
skinny lambs. They nudged my hands and began bleating
loud enough to drown my laughter. Their long rope like
tails wriggled vigorously.

"I'm glad you came. I knew you would." It was William.

"Look!" he said, holding out a couple of tiny, bloodied
fleeces, neatly cut and still damp. "The jacket skins of two
dead lambs. Let's see if the mothers will accept them."

He pulled some catgut and a harness needle from his
pocket, threaded the needle and knelt beside me. Laying
one pelt on the floor, he wrapped the other across the
back of the lamb whose head I had just been fondling. He
gripped the lamb between his knees; its back legs barely
touching the floor, front legs sticking awkwardly straight
out, and began stitching the little jacket where there should
have been buttons.

Poor *oen bach*! When the one was done, it reminded me

of a picture I had once seen of a wolf in sheep's clothing. I hoped the mother would be fooled into accepting this orphan as her own. As William finished, I wondered how he would know which pelt should belong to which mother.

"Wait and see," he said handing me a lamb to carry. "Here! You take one."

I held the lamb close to my chest. It went quiet as we walked out of the kitchen into the wind and nuzzled against me for warmth. William led the way. He lifted the latch of the shippon and turned his shoulder against the door to force it open. It was very dark inside and my eyes took a while to adjust. Light came from three slim, slit windows, close to the eaves of the roof where the wind blew in. You could hear it trying to whistle foreign songs. The shippon was small and the entire floor was covered with straw.

Two ewes lifted their heads and stood to their feet as we came in. Their rumination turned to deep throated 'baas' and we put the lambs down on the straw.

"Watch!" said William, stepping back and fixing the latch on the door. Both the lambs approached the bigger ewe, bleating loudly. They butted her looking for milk. She stepped sideways and turned her head to sniff them, while calling for her lost lamb. Sniffing the one, she began licking it and then stopped to very roughly butt the other lamb away from her. She turned her body to accept the chosen lamb, allowing it to suckle. His tail began wriggling with delight.

"That's one," William whispered. The other ewe had moved in curiosity towards the rejected lamb. It was bleating pathetically, standing helpless in the middle of the shippon. Its legs looked too long for its body, stationed widely apart. The little thing looked as if it might topple over at any minute. She sniffed and turned her head away disinterested. The lamb bleated desperately.

"No!" My heart whispered in equal desperation and I crouched down on my haunches, willing the lamb to move towards the ewe.

"Go on!" I whispered out loud. William crouched beside me. The movements of his feet in the straw made the ewe turn. Still ruminating she 'baa-ed' at him in defiance. He smiled back.

"Go on, *baban*, she hasn't got a heart of stone. Go on! Closer!" he whispered. In response, the tentative thing took steps towards the sour-faced ewe and bleated even louder.

"She'll accept him eventually. Let's leave them and I'll come and see how they're doing later." William stood and unlatched the door. I was disappointed we weren't going to watch until the end of the story.

"Come on Elin. I've got something to show you." He reached into a dark recess in the stone behind the door and pulled out what looked a like a winnowing basket or a cockle sieve, but the mesh was too fine.

"I came to see the lambs," I protested.

He answered with a grin, put his hand on my shoulder and gently pushed me outside.

"I'll show you." He laughed and ran, leaving me to follow him round the shippon and up through the dried bracken. We weren't going to hunt lambs. I knew that. I had followed him enough times on his crackpot mining ventures up the mountainside. He said we were prospectors.

Beyond the bracken, we were scrambling over the jutting granite boulders and scuffing dust between winter worn clumps of heather. Confident, agile and lithe, William led while I lagged a minute behind. When I pulled myself up by the tufts of heather my hand was aching again. Ever since Dad had smacked it back against the privy wall, for pulling beets instead of potatoes, my hand ached when the weather changed. Today spring was in the air.

William had reached a level ridge and began to drop down into the valley of the *nant*. I ran up across the heather so I wouldn't lose him, although I knew these mountains as well as he did. Carreg Du stood seemingly protective on our left, the highest and proudest of our mountains, watching us climb. I reached the ridge and looked down at the nant. It ran frothing around the rocks in agitation as if it had lost its way and was trying to get from the exposed barren rocks to the shelter of the trees further down the valley.

The *nant* ran with many moods. In the spring it was erratic, sometimes swelling high with rain and meltwater and sometimes almost running dry. In the summer it was cool and more consistent but thin in comparison to the winter. We had come here in the summer. I had unbuttoned my boots, removed my stockings and paddled, splashing William in jest until you couldn't tell sweat from river water in his hair.

I climbed down into the valley and out of the wind.

"William, where are these lambs?"

He stopped and waited for me to catch up with him. When I got close enough I could see the laughter dancing in his eyes.

He leaned towards me and whispered, "Can you keep a secret?"

"Of course, I can!" I had kept many secrets with fourteen years of practice.

William's laughter ricocheted off the rocks. Not knowing why, I laughed back.

"So what is it? Copper?" I asked.

"No! It's much more exciting than that. Come on, Elin, I'll show you."

And he set off ahead of me again with that basket thing still tucked under his arm. I followed close behind up the gully of the *nant*. It got narrower and narrower to where there was a miniature waterfall trickling into a pool. William stood above it and ran his hand through the water while holding the winnowing basket in the flow. He was staring intensely at the basket and disturbing the water above the waterfall. Then, he pulled the winnowing basket out from the flow of water and bent his face closer to it. He sifted it first one way and the next, tilting the layer of silt that had collected on the bottom of the mesh. With a grin, he stuck his finger in like little Tommy Tucker sticking his thumb in a plum pudding, and picked up something tiny, squished between his finger and thumb. He lifted it right in front of my eyes. I went cross-eyed.

"Look, Elin! Look!" he said in an awe-inspired whisper. I frowned and pulled my head back so I could focus on his dirty fingers. There was nothing interesting to see: a bit of mud?

"Look in the light," he said, moving his hand to see if he could catch a bit of sunlight. The sun! Where was the sun? How long had it been gone? My stomach tripped over itself and William mistook my gasp for understanding.

"You see it?" he asked. "Isn't it amazing?"

"No!" I said with panic cracking my voice. "The sun has gone. We need to go." We had been too long with the orphan lambs to leave enough time for the mountains and now the sun had disappeared behind them.

William turned from studying his finger to study my face and, at that moment, I saw a tiny glint of reflection in the silt he held. I reached out and pulled his hand towards me. I could see it.

"No!" I whispered. "It can't be."

"It is!" He barely mouthed the words. "Isn't it amazing?"

"It can't be." I looked closer in disbelief. So tiny and shiny, it could be anything, a scrap of metal, a tiny gem, a speck of sand or just a coincidence.

"But it is, Elin." He looked pained. He rummaged in his sieve again and showed me another glint.

"It is!" he insisted. "Look! Another—I always find it here."

"No, William." I shook my head. "It can't be real."

He looked at me. I was unfamiliar with arguing with William. It was as if I had spat at him.

"Come, we must go." I said looking up. "The sun's gone. I'm going to get into trouble. We must run." And then, I couldn't help myself. "It's a foolish hope, William. It can't be real treasure."

My words hit him like a slap. He didn't move while I began to climb back up the craggy boulders straight out of the gully rather than the way we had come. Going up was easier than down. I had not gone far before William climbed beside me. As I reached for the corner of a rock to haul myself up, he caught my wrist. Unsmiling now, he held my aching hand very firmly. I winced. He wasn't to know how much it hurt.

"Not a word to anyone, you understand?"

I understood.

"Whatever you think, Elin, it's a secret," he insisted. I caught a hint of anger in his voice.

I bit my lip and nodded. I know! I can keep secrets.

He loosened his hold. I flexed my wrist and rubbed my hand.

"I won't say anything. I promise!"

"I'll make you rich," he joked. We were back on familiar terms. I laughed at him.

"I don't want to be rich. I just want to get home without getting into trouble."

The valley below was in shadow. We pulled ourselves up into the wind on the top of the ridge above the *nant*, and ran. Through the springy heather and bracken the wind whipped and beat us all the way home. At the farm, I collected some butter from Mrs Gruffudd and ran on alone.

It was dark when I got home. To avoid being reprimanded I went around the back and in through the kitchen door. The scullery was dark and empty. I could see Ifan's figure silhouetted by the light of the front room. He was standing in the doorway with his back to me. As I put the butter down on the slate, a voice I did not know spoke from the front room. I crept forward and peeped around

Ifan. It was Mr Parry with his son, Rhodri, looking out of place in our cottage.

Chapter Four

The next morning, Ifan sat hunched in a chair by the range.

"Where's Dad?" I asked.

"He's gone to speak to Mr Parry and he'll come for me on his way back."

That was serious. That meant a cut in pay.

"But Mr Parry was here last night. What's going on, Ifan?"

"Ceinwen's been seen walking out."

"Walking out?"

"Yes, you know, courting. Mr Price, Gweinidog told Mam the other day that Ceinwen had been seen walking out with Rhodri Parry."

"Rhodri Parry?" I was shocked. "Courting Ceinwen? Is that why the Parry's came last night? He hasn't asked to marry her, has he?"

"No." Ifan smiled. "Quite the opposite. Dad was angry. He told Mam that Ceinwen thinks too highly of herself, above her station and lots of choice words you don't need to know. There have been rumours going around the *caban*, bits of gossip. Rhodri came with his Dad, last night, to tell our Dad that they aren't true."

"What? None of them? Has she been walking out with him? Are they courting?"

"She has been walking out with him but I got a little

confused, to be honest. I think they have been walking together but not courting. He said something about the chapel in Trem y Mynydd and that they had been going to the revival meetings together." He shook his head. "I can't imagine that. It doesn't sound like Ceinwen; her going to something like that—all emotion and hysteria from what I have heard in the *caban*. She's got her head screwed on and her feet on the ground. She wouldn't go to something like that."

"So why has Dad gone to see Mr Parry today?" I asked.

Ifan wasn't sure. He said that Dad had said he needed to see Mr Parry, the engineer, about something to do with Mr Price, Gweinidog.

"Was he still angry about Ceinwen, though?" I asked him.

"Yes. He's been on the verge of a fight with anyone in the *caban* who even mentions Ceinwen's name. He's a proud man, Elin."

"Elin!" Mam called from the back door.

"*Bore da*, Mam," I greeted her.

"The boat comes in today. Will you stop by Mr Hughes and remind him about my sack of flour?"

I stood in the doorway to the back room and saw her wrapping a hot *tatws* in a rag. She handed it to me.

"Yes, Mam." I put it in my basket with my slate and waited as she wrapped another for Ifan and one for Dad.

"Good girl. Here, *cariad*." The warmth of the potatoes seeped through the rags into my hand. I gave Ifan his.

"*Diolch*."

Mam stood in the doorway, wiping her floured hands on her apron. She had been preparing the bread again.

23

"Come Elin. Time to go."

Outside, the wind pulled hard at my plaits and teased, slapping my cheeks, bringing colour to them. It was cold, fresh and clear; another dry day. The wind, pushing in from the sea and bluffing and laughing around the valley, was making the uneasy white horses on the waves ride high and distorting the sound of the quarry gear on the incline. The school bell rang. I ran across the green.

All morning, we sat in silent, tidy rows with two to a desk and eight to a form. The schoolroom had been built before the terrace of houses and wasn't quite big enough for the number of children attending now. We recited by rote, read and added our sums. Miss Evans instructed us in a monotone. I daydreamed. It was so much easier to lose myself in my imaginings than to concentrate on lessons.

I imagined lush green islands, bleak but beautiful with space to run and no one to tell me what to do. I imagined a big white house with shining windows and a life of leisure for the lady in it. I imagined sun shining in at the library window and a grand piano being played, the melody swelling out across the lawn. I imagined a life lived by being a mine owner. It was luxury and ease earned by the sweat and toil of quarrymen the landowner never saw.

William dreamed of mines. He worked for my Uncle John now, but he dreamt of finding a fortune in the rocks, one day.

I imagined a life in a valley where there was no death and I would not leave Mam at the cemetery gate to grieve for her babies. I had listened when Miss Evans talked with pride, to inspire us girls that there was more to life than the quarry, but we were unlikely to ever leave the valley.

There was talk of quarrymen putting money aside for a college in Bangor but that wasn't for girls.

My dreams were pure daydreams; little changed. Young men moved away—more often these days—and the postman brought news on his bicycle from over the mountain. He and the weekly boat were our bridge to another world.

We heard the horn herald the ship coming in, and the fidgeting began, until Miss Evans said we could go. We stood. She prayed. "Amen," we chorused. As the door opened the wind hurtled in, lifting the volume of our voices, and we changed from speaking English to Welsh.

Mr Price, Gweinidog came out of the double doors of the chapel and watched the scattered procession from the schoolroom clatter past his sanctuary. Every Wednesday, every week it was the same—a half day of school and the ship from Liverpool in at the quay—but somehow it never lost its novelty. Every week it was just as exciting, with all the mysteries of the outside world coming to bring news and goods and untold possibilities into our rough, exposed harbour.

I stopped by the shop in the village to give Mr Hughes Mam's message and then headed on home.

Chapter Five

After chapel, the following Sunday, William caught me outside before we went home. He pulled a handkerchief from his pocket and unfolded it.

"Look, Elin."

On the white cloth were tiny particles of gold, lots of them, a bit bigger than dust, like crumbs.

Ifan was with his friend, Gareth Thomas, and Mam had already left to go visiting on her way home. Remembering I had promised to keep it a secret, I turned my back on Mr Price, Gweinidog and Miss Evans talking together in the door of the chapel and grinned at William.

"Amazing! You have found some more."

They did look like bits of gold, but not from our valley, surely?

"What have you got there, William?" Mr Price strode across to us.

"Oh, nothing important, sir." William was quick to fold the handkerchief and put it back in his pocket.

Mr Price turned to me.

"Elin, Miss Evans says you need help learning your recitation. I would be glad to help you."

I thanked him and he suggested a time to practise at the Manse. William went up the hill. I walked home across the green. Gold? William had found gold. Those particles looked more like I expected gold to look than the speck he had shown me in the river.

The cottage door was open. Dad was home. He rarely went to chapel, only when someone died or got married. But it wasn't Dad.

"Ceinwen," I squealed, and leapt across the room.

"Of course! It's Mothering Sunday. I didn't think you'd come."

"Now why did you think that, *oen bach*?"

"I didn't think you would ever have time to come back and see us."

She smiled at me. Ifan came in, shutting the door behind him.

"Where's Mam?" Ceinwen asked.

"She stopped by to see Mrs Roberts and her new baby." Ifan told her. "How are you?"

Ceinwen didn't answer. Twins; they communicate with their eyes.

"*Ble mae Dad?*" she asked instead.

A dark look passed between them. Ceinwen shuddered and nothing else was said.

"What's this? Simnel cake? How exciting! One, two, three, four, five, six, seven, eight, nine, ten, yes!"

Eleven apostles sat on top, shaped in round balls of marzipan. No Judas, the betrayer!

"I made it for Mam," Ceinwen said.

Trust Ceinwen! I rubbed my hands together. Come on home now Mam, I thought. You will love this surprise— Ceinwen here with her simnel cake.

Ceinwen looked different. I watched her lift the kettle off the range and fill the tea pot. Her hair swept up on top of her head, neat and natural, made her look more grown up. It was strange how it only felt like a few weeks since she had left here to work as an under laundry maid at Plas Horon. In truth, she had been gone for months. Now her hands were peeling in places with red lines between the dry patches. She disappeared and came back to the rattle of tea cups. I caught Ceinwen's hand as she put the cups down and held it between mine. It was rough.

"Do they hurt?"

"Sometimes," she said. "But it's no matter."

"I can get some lanolin from Mrs Gruffudd for you, if you want it."

"Ah, I've missed you, Elin." She hugged me close.

I pressed myself into her firm body, my ear next to her heart. I had missed her too.

BANG!

The door flew open and we jumped apart. Dad stood there swaying.

"Ceinwen," he bellowed, loud enough for every cottage in the valley to hear.

She stepped forward readying herself to receive her welcome home, but stopped. The sweet reek of fermented malt blew in the breeze, preceding him. He blinked and winked. His eyes were red, like he had been crying. She stepped back, fluttered like the sail of a ship turned into the wind and sank into the chair by the range, with her back to him. In an instant, Ifan rose and stood sentinel between Dad and Ceinwen.

"Dad!" he exclaimed.

"Out of my way, fool." Dad strode towards Ifan, his arms swinging clumsily.

"ALED!"

Dad stopped and turned very slowly. He blinked at the sunlight and swayed again. There was Mam. For a minute she stood silhouetted in the open door frame before her clogs clapped across the slates. She grabbed Dad's beard with both hands and pulled his face towards hers.

"It's the Sabbath. And look at you—a Holy mess." Her voice, high pitched, cracked as she let his head go back with a rough shove, her fists balled.

He rolled back and swung round on Ceinwen.

"It's *her* fault."

"What?" Ceinwen looked to Ifan. "What have I done?" Ifan didn't look at her. There was silence.

"*Putain!*" Dad spat suddenly and lunged towards Ceinwen but Mam grabbed his hand and pulled him so he stumbled and crumpled onto the flags, like a baby misjudging its first steps. He looked up bewildered.

Standing over him with her hands on her hips, Mam chastised him.

"She is not!"

Fair white, Ceinwen looked to me for help. I stared back blank. Dad was drunk. Whatever he said did not make any sense.

"You were right!" she said to me. "I shouldn't have come." She stood up, stepped around Dad, kissed Mam on the cheek, grabbed her hat and shawl and was gone.

No one spoke. Dad sat on the floor. Ifan stood still, soldier straight. Mam looked at the table all laid out and wilted.

"Ceinwen," she called in anguish out of the door. "Oh, Ceinwen." She turned sadly into the room.

"It's *your* fault, Aled." She dropped into the chair and threw a disgusted look across at her husband in a heap on the floor.

It was one of those storms. I didn't wait to see what was

going to happen next. I didn't want to see Mam cry and Dad shout. I ran.

"Ceinwen?"

Where was she? I had to find her. She had come all the way over from Plas Horon to see us and after only a few minutes was gone. It was not right. I glanced through the people who were still standing on the green, talking after chapel. She wasn't there. I ran past the shop and looked down on the pebble-ridged beach. The tide was out. A few trousered figures ambled along the strip of sand or clambered on the pebbles, but there was no Ceinwen skirting the edge.

I turned back and began heading up towards the schoolroom and chapel. Maybe she would go to the farm? Maybe she would see Uncle John before going back? She had come so far for so little. I reached the track to Nant Uchaf before I saw her: a lone figure, winding through the bracken on the path that led to the track along the edge of Carreg Du. She was going back to Plas Horon.

I ran. I scrambled. I panted. Eventually, I called out and reached her as the path met the track. She waited for me, the wind whispering at loose strands of her hair. Even from below, I could see that her face was blotchy with swollen strawberry patches on her cheeks.

"Elin, *cariad*," she said.

Standing panting on the track, I rested my hands on my knees, leant forward and sucked the valley into my lungs. I don't think I'd ever climbed that path so fast.

"What was all that about? What does Dad think I have done?"

I had not got the breath to speak. My lungs felt as if they had been scrubbed inside with dried heather and my head as if it had been whisked like cream.

"Why, on the one day when I get to come home and see Mam? It was supposed to be her day. But Dad! You know, he has to spoil it. What have I done, Elin?" She fixed her bright, blue eyes on mine and answered her own question.

"Nothing! That's what—I have done nothing to upset Dad. I have not even been here."

She was cross. I stood up straight and stretched the ache out of my muscles.

"I don't know, Ceinwen. It's just Dad. He has been drinking. You know what he's like. Ifan did say Dad has been very angry of late."

"That's Dad, it hasn't got anything to do with me."

It felt like spreading rumours of rumours and telling tales as I stumbled over my words and tried to explain.

"Ifan told me that Mam said Mr Price had told her you had been seen walking out with Rhodri Parry. Dad thinks that means you must be courting. It made him angry. Ifan said Dad thinks you are getting above yourself. He went to see Mr Parry and the other night Mr Parry and Rhodri came round. So maybe it was to do with you?"

All colour faded from her face, even the strawberry patches bled white. She didn't say anything for a few moments while the wind teased the wayward hairs around her face.

"Oh no!" she faltered. "Oh Lord," she sniffled. "I wonder what was said?"

"So you're not walking out with Rhodri?"

"No!" she insisted.

"Oh!" she said in a shadowy hush. "Even if I was, Dad would make it his business to spoil everything. He overreacts." And then they came. Tears fell. I watched her

31

and waited. Ceinwen wiped her nose and looked north-west up the track that would lead to Plas Horon and her position of service. She put an arm around my shoulder and turned me south-east.

"I think I have overreacted too," she said sadly. "Come."

We began walking the track. In silence, we trekked. I wanted to ask where we were going but didn't. We weren't going back home. She was lost in sniffs and gulps, wiping snot and tears with one of the cotton handkerchiefs Mam had given her when she left home.

The track wound round Carreg Du towards Trem y Mynydd. The trees grew thick where it converged with the road out of Nant. It felt colder in the shadows. I didn't have my coat or shawl. When we came out into the sunshine again we were sheltered from the wind by the mountain.

Someone was coming up behind us. I could hear hooves catching and scattering stones on the track, the rattle of a bridle and heavy revolution of a metal-rimmed wheel trundling. The horse was trotting so we stepped up on to the grass verge out of the way and turned to watch the cart pass.

The cart came closer and I recognised the pony at the same time as I heard a voice I knew call out.

"*Helo! Sut wyt ti?*"

Uncle John reined in the pony and I stepped forward to hold her bridle. Blodyn softly blew on my face with her velvet nose and I blew back into her nostrils. She knew me. Last summer, Uncle John had let me ride her bareback, like a boy, when he was taking her up to the farm after she had been working. She was a black cob that Uncle John had always been proud of. He threw a foal from her every other year, to help her earn her keep, but she was worth more than money to him. She was steady and dependable. I kissed her on the softest sweet spot above her nostril.

"Would you like a lift?" Uncle John asked. Mrs Gruffudd was smiling down her beak-like nose at me from her perch beside him and I smiled back, uncertainly.

"*Diolch*," Ceinwen said, lifting down the chained tailgate of the cart. I looked at Uncle John. He was amused.

"Come on, Elin. Hop on." He nodded a nudge to me to get in. I left Blodyn and clambered up beside Ceinwen, with our feet on the tailgate, we faced back looking at the place where the tracks met.

"So, she persuaded you to come, did she, Elin?" Uncle John cheerfully threw the question over his shoulder at us.

"Well, no!" I answered back. "I don't know where we're going."

Uncle John rumbled with laughter which brought a smile to Ceinwen's face.

"Oh! That's beautiful." He looked back and crossed glances with Ceinwen. She absently began to scrutinise the paisley pattern on her shawl with her finger. I saw Uncle John look at her again long enough to trace the tears. He glanced at me in a silent question mark.

"Dad," I mouthed.

He nodded. And we continued on in silence, Blodyn's steady hoofbeats echoing in the landscape and marking time with the drone of the wheels turning. Occasionally, one of the wheels would catch a stone. They pinged and jumped out from under the metal rim to hit the verge. Blodyn snorted in contentment.

On reaching Trem y Mynydd we met people strolling in

all directions. Uncle John and Mrs Gruffudd greeted those going in the same direction as us. There were so many; anyone would think it was the summer fayre. Blodyn stopped.

"Well, girls—down you get," he said. He smiled at Mrs Gruffudd. We slipped off the back and she stepped down from the front, taking her Bible in her hand. I held Blodyn's head while Uncle John climbed down, folded the reins in his hands and tucked them into her harness. We lead her to an open bit of grassland that was bordered by a drainage ditch. Beyond was the rough scrub of heather and bracken. Uncle John undid the traces and breeching, and pushed the cart back releasing Blodyn from the shafts. He rested them on a grassy mound of earth and, removing much of the harness, tethered the pony to graze.

"From here we walk," he said, smiling at me. "There, girl." He rubbed Blodyn's neck affectionately and we left her.

I looked up the road into town. People had dispersed and Ceinwen and Mrs Gruffudd had disappeared. The excitement of the town had hidden itself in some sanctified secret. Where was everyone?

"Now tell me, Elin," Uncle John said, confidentially taking my arm, "What has happened? What's upset your sister?"

"Dad's been drinking. Ceinwen came home for Mother's Day and Ifan says Dad's cross with her. Mam was told that she's been seen walking out with Rhodri Parry, but she says she's not." I turned to him. "It's all a mess. Mam's cross with Dad now and Ceinwen reckons Dad wrecks everything. I think they're all feeling very sore and cross."

"And you, Elin *bach*?"

We walked on.

Yes! And me! I held my tender wrist. Dad was so unpredictable. I was cross with him too for spoiling what should have been a happy day. I was cross with him for upsetting Mam and Ceinwen. Uncle John was different. He had a unique way of making you feel like he understood you and that you were special. He didn't judge. You didn't have to behave in a certain way to feel accepted by him. He accepted you as you were.

Up the steps we went, with the dusk behind us. Uncle John reached forward and wrenched the solid chapel door open. Inside, it was overflowing with people, illuminated by light that made them burnish. So this was where everyone had hidden themselves. I looked around for Ceinwen. There were so many people and so many unfamiliar faces. Why hadn't she waited for me?

People were sitting hunched forward. Some were on their knees. Every head was bowed. They looked timeless and ageless, oblivious of anyone around them. The hushed silence cushioned me and I squashed beside Uncle John on a spare square of one of the pews at the back, beneath the gallery. Was this the hysteria that Ifan had spoken of? It didn't seem very hysterical. It felt peaceful and comforting.

I copied Uncle John and leant forward but kept my eyes open for a sneak peek around the room. The last time I had been in this chapel was for Uncle John's wedding and then I had sat at the front beneath the *sêt fawr* looking up at the minister. Owen had been sick. The twins had been reprimanded for giggling. I remembered how I had swung my legs sitting on the pew and had dropped my ribbons but wasn't allowed to pick them up. It had been the first time Dewi had seen Mared. Llinos had looked so radiant, she outshone the bride. When I saw Llinos more recently, she looked wrung out and forgotten, with crow's feet stamping the light out of the corner of her tired eyes and her face so beaten by the weather. My poor big sister; Mam had said she was weak as a baby but beautiful. She had learnt to fight when life was difficult and still she fought on.

The chapel felt smaller than I remembered, too. Mind you, Uncle John had been married for a good long time now. Owen was just a boy when his new stepmother, Jane, came into his life and now he was a man, almost ready to have his own home. It was little wonder he was sick on their wedding day. A new mother would have been a daunting prospect but Mrs Gruffudd, his step mother, was lovely. I had always liked her. She and Uncle John had made the farm into a special place, a haven, and one of the first places we would go when trouble was brewing. Their home was always open and hospitable.

Today the chapel felt smaller, not just because I had grown, but because it seemed to be labouring under a great weight of people. The minister was in the *sêt fawr* but he neither faced the congregation nor stood. He knelt. Mr Price never conducted a service from his knees. We all stood in our chapel, the way you should. Mind you, Mr Price read from a book with a singsong voice that was easy to shut out and instead watch bluebottles dying on the windowsill or lose myself in my imaginings. This was different. What was going on? It really did feel like we had just walked into something that had been going on for hours.

Someone was speaking. I searched for the voice. I could

hear a crescendo of feminine muttering, rising. It was
going somewhere, gathering momentum. Then it flared
with clarity and I distinguished her cry,
  "*Arglwydd, Arglwydd!*"
She reminded me of a seagull. I had spotted the speaker
at the furthest point from me in the chapel. She was
standing with her arms raised, her voice soaring. People
around me were nodding and exclaiming. Their *amens* kept
her going, rising on the thermal of agreement. Maybe this
was a touch of hysteria? As she came to the climax of
her prayer a song burst out of the gallery. Again it was a
woman. My teacher, Miss Evans, would be pleased to see
women taking a lead, only she might disapprove that it was
in chapel.

People shuffled to their feet and joined in. Uncle John's
rich bass harmonised, undulating against the melody. It
was beautiful. The sound filled the room with an aurora
of warmth. Cradled in peace, I stayed sat down, closed my
eyes and listened, resting back against the stiff panel of
the chapel pew. I picked out the high and pure sounds in
the myriad of voices. I could hear the sonorous and low.
It sounded like thousands of tongues. I was sure there
were more people in the room than I could see. Although
I wanted to sing too, I didn't know the words so I let the
melody bubble up in a hum.

It was when I opened my eyes that I saw Ceinwen. She
wasn't singing but was on her knees weeping. Her face
was lifted, her eyes were shut and she was glowing. Tears
glistened on her cheeks. I watched her open her eyes
and a rush of tears fell down her face. She smiled a wide
clean fresh washed smile. No longer sad or confused, she
seemed transported to another land, in a dream.

More people were praying. One thing seemed to flow into another, a song, a prayer, a promise. The past and the future seemed irrelevant. It was just here and now. No one was leading. Then all ceased. A blanket of heavy silence fell as people returned to their seats and expectancy buzzed from heart to heart and mind to mind. People sat waiting, eyes closed and patient.

I did not want to open my eyes. But curiosity got the better of me. What was everyone waiting for? What were they doing? I opened one eye and peeped. A boy rose slowly to his feet on the front row and cried out.

"Lord, forgive me!" Even through that penitent sound I recognised his voice. It was William.

Chapter Six

William? What had come over him? I was uncomfortable—so I shuffled. Uncle John sat statue-still beside me. I looked at Ceinwen. She was motionless too, listening. I stared harder. She was not even breathing. No one stepped forward to hush him. They let him cry out. What a strange service! William had forgotten his dignity and everyone else had turned to stone. Maybe the clock had stopped too? My heart hammered heavily on my eardrum.

I listened to William. A sinner, he said? No! He was not a sinner. Dad was. He drank and it made him bad. He did not go to chapel. Sinners were people like that. They drank and gambled, hit their wives, had babies when they were not married and stayed away from chapel. William was none of those. He was good and kind. He cared for those sheep with gentleness and compassion. Maybe William thought it was sinful to find gold or to want to be a mine owner? Wasn't it one of the Ten Commandments not to covet, not to want what belonged to someone else? Maybe William thought wanting what he hadn't got was sin? He wasn't a sinner.

People were rising now, dotted around the room like the round hut ruins of Tre'r Ceiri. Then they swooped down on William. Mrs Gruffudd was amongst them. What were they going to do to him? I'll defend you, William. I imagined rushing forward to push back those people. Get back you! Don't touch him. He is innocent. He is not a sinner. But I did not move. Very gracefully, they encircled him, a cloud around him obscuring my view. Gentle murmurs whispered a mystery to me. What were they saying? Grace? Forgiveness? More tears were glistening on people's cheeks. They looked so contented. Uncle John wordlessly mouthed beside me, like a sheep ruminating. He had his eyes firmly closed in prayer. I could not hear what he said. I guess God could. What a lot of people God had to listen to all at once, but somehow it sounded like a song, almost a chorus of prayer.

The minister had risen and was standing facing the congregation with an arm stretched forward towards the great cloud of people. His arm rose slightly and fell with the motion of his praying and then, as if he had conducted the wave of prayer to be still, people began to drift back to their seats.

"I tell you that in the same way there will be more rejoicing in heaven over one sinner who repents than over ninety-nine righteous persons who do not need to repent." (Luke 15:7)

This verse he spoke like a fanfare while beaming down on everyone from the *sêt fawr*. But William wasn't a sinner, I was sure of that.

"Croeso William. The Lord has heard your prayer. *Mae ef gyda chi."* Then to the congregation he trumpeted the words,

"Consecrate yourselves, for tomorrow the LORD *will do amazing things among you."* (Joshua 3:5)

He spoke for a long time then, saying something about

us being in an important place like the Israelites were, when they crossed the Jordan. We must follow, he said. He kept going on about the nation and that the Lord was doing something wonderful, taking the nation across the Jordan. I did not understand. He said we should pick up stones as we crossed the Jordan that would tell of the amazing things God had done among us so we would remember to tell our children. I just kept thinking about William. He wasn't a sinner.

Then, I couldn't help myself. I indulged in my escape trick into the world of imagination. Maybe it was a sin to use your imagination? My thoughts soon wandered and I was remembering climbing amongst the stones and boulders behind the quarry, with William, and looking out at the tiny kingdoms of Ireland and *Ynys Môn*. The sun was shining, the sky deep, cloudless blue. The sea was a looking glass image of splendour on either side of the peninsula as the land and sandy beaches wriggled away towards Bardsey. Whether we were sinners or not this was God's land. He made it. He ruled it. I knew God was in it, when we climbed the mountains. Can you hear *me*, I wondered. Did He actually care to listen to me? He was the invisible God who was everywhere. Could He hear me?

The minister kept saying Joshua three, the third chapter of the book of Joshua. Perhaps God would speak to me through the minister? We were to follow and obey wherever God led us, he was saying.

"He will do amazing things among you."

What amazing things was God going to do? Increase Dad and Ifan's pay? Bring Mam's lost babies back to life? Help William establish a gold mine? I was good at imagining but somehow I couldn't imagine what God could do.

"The LORD bless you and keep you; the LORD make his face shine on you and be gracious to you; the LORD turn his face towards you and give you peace." (Numbers 6:24–26)

The minister dismissed us, yet no one moved. I twisted my head restlessly wondering what was next. Uncle John put his hand over mine and smiled peace to me. Some people began to rustle and rise, re-pinning hats or picking up caps, coats and shawls, others sat passively, tarrying. Again the gallery began singing a celebration and people began to navigate towards the door. By the third chorus, Mrs Gruffudd was at my shoulder, her firebird eyes aflame beneath the red feathers of her hat.

"Where is Ceinwen?" I asked her.

She turned and looked across the room as an answer. Ceinwen was amongst a group of youngsters of similar fresh-skinned complexion, either clean shaven or with peaches and cream cheeks. She was animated and happy, chatting to a girl beside her. She looked so different from the crushed and confused girl I came with. She looked refreshed.

"We'll take you home, Elin. Ceinwen will go back to Plas from here." Uncle John was saying to me. "She comes every Sunday."

Every Sunday?—Really? I hadn't meant to come to chapel. I didn't know we were going. It had all been a mistake, but Ceinwen chose to come here every Sunday. Could today hide any more surprises?

"Can I say goodbye to Ceinwen first, please?"

He nodded and I tangled my way through the Sunday best dresses and coats until I reached her. Ceinwen had seen me coming and reached for my hand, drawing me into her circle and introducing me to her friends. They all worked on the Plas Horon Estate with her: another laundry maid, a gardener, a groom, a tenant farmer, a scullery maid, a carpenter—these were her companions.

"We walk back together," she told me and laughingly pointed to the gardener. "Huw leads in song all the way."

His already ruddy cheeks went *piws* as she singled him out.

"Go, *oen bach*. And give my love to Mam and Dad," she whispered in my ear as she hugged me goodbye.

"And Dad?"

"Yes, and Dad."

"But—" I didn't understand.

"He is forgiven," she said.

She seemed so different suddenly. I could see she had her own way of life to lead away from our family. I turned back just before we went out of the chapel door. Rhodri Parry was standing with a hand on her shoulder. As I watched, he said something and she laughed. She was happy.

I, on the other hand, was tired. No one spoke and Blodyn plodded back down to the valley towards the tang of salt and seaweed. When Mrs Gruffudd had stepped down at the farm, Uncle John let me sit beside him. He had wrapped my shoulders with a blanket before we began our descent and I was glad. It was cold in the valley. A rumble of sea mist must have come in with the dusk and now shrouded everything. I shivered.

Uncle John set me down outside our door and blessed me. I thanked him for bringing me home and stood to watch him reverse Blodyn. He was a blur of shadow in the mist before I realised I still had his blanket around my shoulders.

In our cottage, the fire was almost out. I looked in the grate. One coal glowed pathetically beneath the rest, so I put the wick of the candle, from the mantelpiece, against it and waited. Suddenly it caught and flamed up, nearly burning my hand. We were not allowed to burn these for long but, for just a moment, I let the light sweep around the room, before putting it in the candle holder. Everything still sat on the table as it had been when I had left. The tea cups, Ceinwen's cake, a jug with milk—these precious things wasted. I climbed the stairs tugging the blanket tight and holding the candle high. Both were a comfort to me.

I passed Dad lying across a bed, fully clad with his boots on, his mouth drooling open; a fluttery rumble vibrated every so often like the wheel at the mill as he breathed in and out. Unflattering, malted dreams washed his face. I didn't want to see. I turned away and left him in the dark.

Where was Mam? Where was Ifan? Of course! It wasn't late. They would be in chapel. The mist had hidden the lights as we came past.

What a strange day it had been, with Ceinwen coming home, Dad's anger, Mam's anger, Ceinwen's flight and my pursuit. But it was stranger still to find that she regularly went to the chapel in Trem y Mynydd where Uncle John went, and that William was there today too. William, who called himself a sinner: William, who could make me laugh, encourage and cheer me up; William, who cared about what I thought and would listen to what I had to say; William, who had aspirations, and made foolish promises of riches to me; William, who always told me things straight and brought the best out of me. He wasn't a sinner. I would follow him wherever he led, but the William I had seen in chapel today, I did not understand.

Shivering, I went to bed, with Uncle John's blanket for warmth. I dreamt I was climbing the mountains on a clear day. I awoke and my heart was pulsing through my mind. It was still dark. I heard the clunk of a foot on the wooden boards and I sat up abruptly.

"Elin?" Ifan half spoke, half whispered. "Are you awake?"

"I am now," I replied. He felt his way across the wooden boards and sat on the edge of the bed pressing my feet flat beside him under the blankets. He leant forward and reached for my cheek. His hand was warm.

"Where did you go?"

"I found Ceinwen."

"Is she all right?"

"She was upset. And Mam?"

"She left after you and went to see Aunt Glenys."

"And you, what did you do?"

"I put Dad to bed. He cried like a child after you and Mam left. It wasn't pretty."

"Ifan, why?"

"I don't know." He sighed—ever gracious—Ifan was concerned for Mam, for Dad, for Ceinwen, for me, but not for himself.

"Where did Ceinwen go?"

I told him about Uncle John and Mrs Gruffudd meeting us on the road, about going to chapel and how Ceinwen had gone back to Plas Horon with her companions. Ifan was also surprised.

"Ceinwen goes to the chapel in Trem y Mynydd?"

"Yes, it seems lots of people do." I didn't want to tell him that I'd seen William there too.

"Mr Price says it is all hysteria and nonsense. I am surprised by Ceinwen. *Dwi wedi fy synnu.*"

"She said she forgave Dad for his meanness to her today. She looked different after chapel, Ifan, you should have seen her. Where's Mam, now?" I asked.

"Downstairs—she asked me to come and see if you were here."

"Has she lit the fire?"

"No. We went back to Aunt Glenys' after chapel. Mam and Aunt Glenys talked a lot about Dad. Aunt Glenys said he was always happy as a boy and a good brother to her but when he worked away from home he was never the same. She doesn't know what happened and it was before Mam knew him. Mam said that she thinks Dad's drinking has got worse recently."

There was a long silence. I'd never known Dad to be any different. It was hard to imagine how he might have been, even as a boy. I looked at Ifan. He had fine chiselled features with high cheek bones. He wasn't very tall but he was strong. Dad might have looked like him except Ifan smiled a lot more.

The air around me was cold. I shivered. Ifan shifted.

"Sleep, *cariad*," he said, standing and lifting the blankets up to my shoulders, encouraging me to snuggle down.

"Ifan." My voice was husky. "I was reminded of Llinos today, in the chapel. It's months since Mam and I went to visit. Do you think it would be all right for me to go and visit her sometime?"

"I'm sure."

"Do you think I could go by myself?"

He smiled.

Now that my legs were long enough to climb the cherry trees and Owen had joked that I would be ready to start work soon, I must be big enough to go alone to visit Llinos. Ifan left and I settled down, ready to sleep. It came sweet, quick and deep. I did not dream again.

Chapter Seven

A little bit of competition and the village was on edge: iron sharpening iron. Everyone was getting flustered with learning their words for the recitation. I was learning Psalm one hundred and seven.

Yna y llefasant ar yr ARGLWYDD yn eu cyfyngder; ac efe a'u gwaredodd o'u gorthrymderau.

Then they cried out to the LORD in their trouble,
and he delivered them from their distress.
(Psalm 107:6)

It was very dramatic. I went to Mr Price for practise, as Miss Evans had suggested, and found myself standing in his red study. It smelt of vinegar and beeswax. A Bible lay open across a leather inlay on the desk. A notebook was also held open by a rough, grey-stone paper weight with a pencil neatly placed beside. The housemaid had called the minister away to someone at the door, so I had a nosey look at his notebook. There was an indistinct pencil sketch. I couldn't tell much by looking at it upside down, but could see a drawing beneath which was written *Iron Pyrites—Fool's Gold.*

Returning footsteps sounded down the hallway. I

straightened and looked at the picture on the wall. An old lady walking in a chapel, devout people praying, kneeling in the pews, she in a paisley shawl and stovepipe hat; *Gweddi* it was called. I liked the old man. He looked sincere. Ifan had told me that the devil's face was in the woman's shawl but I could not see it and I had looked so many times to find it. I just could not see it. It was supposed to symbolise how the devil could go to chapel disguised in the garments of someone religious.

"Tick, tock," the patient clock echoed the steps. I glanced at its numbered face. Ten past ten and the door opened.

"*Mae'n ddrwg da fi, Elin.*"

Mr Price sat. The leather creaked as he crossed his legs, rested his elbows on the arm rests and folded his hands.

"Now, begin again."

And so I did. He listened with his two forefingers resting together on his moustached lip.

"*Y neb sydd ddoeth, ac a gadwo hyn, hwy a ddeallant drugareddau yr* ARGLWYDD." *(Psalm 107:43)*

I concluded. Watching his face, I waited. He wasn't much older than my brother Dewi who had gone to work at Penrhyn when he got married. He and Mared had three little ones now, and another on the way. Mr Price wasn't married. He had small eyes. Maybe that was why he wasn't married. No one liked his small eyes. I would like to get married one day. He was frowning and his eyes seemed even smaller.

"Why Psalm one hundred and seven?" He shrewdly pursed his lips.

"I like it."

49

"You *like* it?"

"Yes. I like the way it sounds. I like the descriptions. "

He nodded. Perhaps too simple an explanation for a learned Oxford man, but he was making an effort to be kind.

"You did well." He paused, thinking. Then came the tutoring, the real instruction—a loud and judgemental "however".

"You need to project your voice a bit more. Put your lips together." His moustache met his beard. "And hum. Mmmmm…" he demonstrated.

I tried.

"Can you feel the back of your lips tickle? Can you feel that the sound…" he rose from behind his desk, his tall, slim, figure looming towards me, "…is coming from down here." He struck his middle with an axe hand.

"This is your diaphragm," he said. "It's a muscle beneath your lungs and that's where we push the sound out from. You must relax it before you begin with deep breaths. Like so… in… out… in… out. Now, try again, my dear."

My dear! I was no more 'dear' to him than the man in the moon. Was Mr Price capable of having affection for anyone?

He sat down. I sighed relief and breathed deeply, gearing myself to speak more clearly.

"*Felly dyweded gwaredigion yr ARGLWYDD, y rhai a waredodd efe o law y gelyn,*" (*Psalm 107:2*). Let the redeemed of the Lord tell their story.

I threw my voice at him, spattering him with the story of the redeemed, their moments of anguish calling on the Lord to rescue them, and how He saved them every time—letting the intensity of my voice climb and then fall in the refrain, how they cried to him and He came to their rescue. I loved the dramatic and the poetic. It was always when I reached that verse about the storm, *"They were glad when it grew calm" (Psalm 107:30)* that I knew I was comfortably on the incline to the end.

It was like that at home too. I was glad when things grew calm and Dad's anger faded. Ifan could not always protect me, Mam or Ceinwen from Dad, but Ifan wasn't afraid to stand up to Dad in his most frightful moments, neither was Mam. There had been no more outbursts from him since Mothering Sunday.

"Da iawn, Elin, da iawn." He nodded his approval. "I am happy with that. Will that do?" he cocked his head and with a chicken-like stare, waited.

There was a knock at the door. The brass knob slowly turned. It was Non, William's older sister. The frills of her mob cap framed her face and she looked ashamed.

"I'm really sorry, Sir," she said, "He says it can't wait."

Grit scratched the wooden floor as Mr Price thrust back his chair. He was gone before the dust could settle.

Non smiled at me.

"How are you getting on?" she asked, kind-eyed.

"Iawn."

I loved the challenge of a recitation. I loved to listen to voices speaking like song, with inflection melodically rising and falling telling the great and wondrous deeds of our God. I loved to enter into the competition of trying to express emotion through words and I loved the long and elaborate words found in the Bible that spoke of a majestic God.

Y neb sydd ddoeth, ac a gadwo hyn, hwy a ddeallant drugareddau yr ARGLWYDD.

Let the one who is wise heed these things
and ponder the loving deeds of the LORD.

(Psalm 107:43)

Non was wise, or so I thought. I'd known her since I was tiny. She was the sort of girl who seemed to think before she spoke, less impetuous than William. She was kind too, very kind. It made her beautiful with a dependable sort of beauty that didn't fade and came from her smiling eyes and quiet way. But today, I did not tell her how much the recitation really meant to me.

"*Iawn,*" I said again.

"William told me you went to see the lambs the other day."

She was one of the few girls to find service and still live at home, and she and William were close, not in age but in friendship.

"I did. We helped some orphans."

"They are skinny when they're first born, aren't they? And so helpless."

"William showed me how he sews jackets on them."

"Oh yes. The old 'Let's Deceive Mother' trick." She sounded like William when she laughed.

"It's amazing when it works."

"Anyhow," Non smoothed her hands across her apron. "I must get on. Nice to see you, Elin, and I hope you do well. He's a good tutor. He's been helping me too. We'll be competing against each other."

She winked at me, turned and went, leaving the door open. Maybe Mr Price was a good tutor but he made me feel inadequate and small.

I looked back into the room. A rod of sunlight was coming through the big sash window and resting on the notebook on the desk. In it, little bits were drifting and glistening. Miss Evans had been telling us about germs, and Lord Lister who helped to preserve the King's life just before he became king. I wondered if these were germs. I could see them dancing in the air. I squinted my eyes to focus on them. They looked like little bits of gold, twinkling.

William and his nonsense secret about gold dust in the mountains! That dust he held in his handkerchief and the bits he found in the *nant*, sometimes I struggled to believe it really was gold. Tin? Yes! Or copper. They had been found before, but not gold. There were gold mines down Barmouth way. I remember hearing Uncle John talking about them once to Owen: something about someone they knew who worked in one, a small one. My memory was vague. But there was nothing around here. The quarry was for granite and there were the slate mines further inland. William had told me, before, that it was tin and copper he hoped to find, not gold. What if he actually has found gold? Mr Price's notebook said something about gold. I stepped behind his desk and looked at the notebook. His calligraphic handwriting was quite beautiful when read the right way up. I could now see the drawing was a pencil replica of the rough stone that I thought was a paper weight. It was dark grey and although the surface was sandpapery it twinkled with tiny flecks that glistened. Yes! *Iron Pyrites—Fool's Gold*, that is what it said, and there was a line pointing to the side of the stone. I looked at the actual stone where the line led to in the drawing and there they were: small crumbs of gold, exactly the same as William had held in his handkerchief. I wanted to pick it up, look closer and feel that rough sand paper surface, but too late, exasperation entered.

"I do wish that man would…" Mr Price saw me. "Elin?"

"Sorry, sir," I withdrew my hand and looked up wide eyed.

"I'm sorry, sir," I said again.

His moustache jigged and wriggled and his little eyes glinted at me.

"Well Elin, you're inquisitive, I suppose," making me feel like a five year old. He picked up the rock.

"I found it in the hills. Iron Pyrites! See those little bits there? They're a sulphide, something to add to my collection. Look! Can you see them?" He pointed. I looked closer, as I had wanted to before, and could see little square structures; a hue of gold. Fondling the rock, Mr Price put it down.

"I found it this morning while I was out on my dawn walk."

A distracted look came over him.

"It's called Iron Pyrites?" I enquired.

"Yes, or Fool's Gold, because it looks like gold. Do you see?"

I nodded. "How do you know it isn't gold?"

"Gold is smoother," he said lifting his head as he spoke, "And a slightly different colour."

I wondered. "Is there much of it in the mountains around here?"

"Oh yes. There's plenty of Fool's Gold. You've probably seen it before and not realised." He smiled without looking at me.

"Have you ever found real gold?"

He looked to the open door as Non passed by.

"Mr Price?" I watched his face. His eyes followed Non's figure and his expression softened. I don't think he had heard me. He never answered my question. But it didn't matter to me. I thought I knew the answer. I rushed through one more rendition of my Psalm for the recitation—Mr Price had forgotten that he had said he was happy with it—and then I shot out into the sunshine and up the hill. I wanted to find William. Gold, or Fool's Gold? Which was it? How would we know the difference?

I found him in the lower pasture bending over a ewe. There were some very newborn lambs bleating to their mothers in the field, not sounding that different from newborn babies.

"Shh!" he hushed me as I approached.

"No noise," he mouthed. "Or you might shock her."

I climbed up onto the top bar of the gate. It was warm in the sun. There was hardly a breath of wind. All in the hedge, the blackthorn was beginning to break. Little white and green tips were starting to show on the jagged twig edges. The flat sea was bright, a mirror, reflecting joy that spring was finally here.

I watched William. He was concentrating wholly on the ewe. She must be a new mother. She was struggling. Her body juddered and she lifted her head, a helpless look at

William. He placed one hand on her flank and the other near her rear. He was talking to her gently, encouraging her all the while. Suddenly he pulled and two stick, black feet protruded. It all happened so quickly before she was licking a shiny black and white baby. All her instincts had kicked in. Proudly, William watched. He wanted to make sure that she was going to be a good mother. Wiping his hands on the grass, he started ambling towards me,

"Well?"

"Well!" I affirmed.

I felt a little sheepish. I had not seen him since chapel on Mothering Sunday. Where should I begin?

He climbed the bottom bars of the gate and looked at me, the sun warming his back.

"What is it?" He tipped his head like the funny little robin that watches me in the vegetable garden.

Now, how was I going to say what I wanted to say? He swung himself around and sat next to me, looking out to sea. Here and there a fishing trawler dotted the smooth surface and bigger boats could be seen drawing lines to and from Ireland and Liverpool. It was so still. I lifted my face and breathed in the sun-soaked, warm air.

"I love this time of year." William spoke quietly. "Even though you don't know what one day from the next will be like, when the sun shines and the wind dies down you know something better is coming. It's like a promise. And it's such a relief from the cold."

These were the words of one who, being out on the mountainside looking after the sheep, had plenty of time to think about and feel the changes of the seasons. I looked at him. He was like David, the shepherd boy, in our

Bible at home. There was a picture at the beginning of the leather bound book that rested on the mantelpiece above the range. It was the only book in the house and was brought down when someone died, got married or there was a new baby—or when we had a passage to learn for recitation. But before I could read, I had sneaked a look in it and found in the front an etched picture of a boy sitting by some sheep with a harp in his hand. The picture stayed in my mind. I couldn't imagine William playing the harp, not like blind Jacob, who went to the blind school for boys in Liverpool. Jacob came back from Liverpool with a beautiful harp and a sweet voice. Now he travelled around creating a cloud of awe and wonder with his harp and song wherever he went.

No! I couldn't see William being like that. He was more like the shepherd in his own joke, who might enjoy a red sky at night but then wake up to find his socks were on fire. William, the shepherd I knew, was impetuous and spontaneous. On the other hand, I had just seen him bring new life into the world. That was significant. Perhaps it required a reflective and melancholic response? I had come to talk to him about his secret gold and instead I was comparing him to King David, harpists and shepherds. This balmy sunshine was going to my head and making me reflective and melancholic too. A bumblebee clumsily blundered around the first blackthorn flower brave enough to open

"Look! A bee," I said pointing. "That's a good sign, if it's warm enough for them…"

"Yes, you should see them busy in the cherry blossom behind the farmhouse."

Of course! In my favourite place, the small orchard was sheltered from the wind behind high stone walls. It was a suntrap and Uncle John kept an apiary there as a perfect sanctuary for insects. They were important workers, for the fruit the orchard produced was famous in the valley. A number of stocky little apple trees were said to have been producing apples for over one hundred and fifty years.

"What did you want to tell me?" William's bright blue-eyed gaze opened the window of my soul: Gold or Fool's Gold. I hung my head and slipped off the gate.

"Come. I want to see the bees and the cherry blossom. I'll tell you as we walk."

He didn't reply, just climbed down and went to open the gate. We started up the track.

"You know this secret of yours?"

"Yes," he looked worried. "You haven't told anyone have you?"

"No. I promised. It's something else. I don't think you've found gold, William."

He paced beside me and waited for me to go on. I looked at my feet moving over the dust and broken bits of rock. My boots were looking scuffed again. They needed some more blacking and dubbin. I must not forget or Mam would have something to say.

"I went to practise my recitation, *yma heddiw* with Mr Price, Gweinidog," I explained. "He has a collection of rocks." I looked up at William. "Did you know that?"

He nodded.

"Yes. Non told me."

"Well, on his desk today was one he had been drawing a picture of, it was *mor fawr â hyn*," I held out my curved

58

hand. "And it was almost black, or at least a dark grey. It was rough on the surface that was cut flat and was full of tiny sparkling bits but on one side were some larger pieces of gold that looked exactly like those you found in the *nant.*"

Illustrating with my hand, I stopped walking and looked at him. He stopped too and turned to face me. I shook my head.

"I really don't think you have found gold, William. It's not gold."

"It is! I am sure it's gold."

"No, it's called *Fool's Gold*. Mr Price said so."

"*Fool's Gold?*"

"Yes! He said gold, *real* gold, looks different. He said *Fool's Gold* is everywhere in the mountains. He reckons we may have seen it without knowing what it is."

An uncertain smile spread across his face and froze as he turned away from me. He frowned. I looked back along the way we had come, following his gaze. There was a man standing down the track, looking out to sea with his back to us. We grimaced at each other. Who is that? The figure was too far away to see.

"I am sure I have found gold."

"But Fool's Gold looks exactly the same as what you showed me," I argued. "Go and see for yourself or ask Non."

He was not listening.

"I am sure that I have found gold," he repeated glancing back again at the man on the track.

There was something about the way he spoke that made me feel ashamed.

"Come on!" he grasped my hand. "Let's go and see the bees."

He'd completely dismissed what I'd said. It was as if it was unimportant. Annoyed, I went with him. As we reached a bend in the track, I looked back. That man was following us but I don't think he had seen us.

In the orchard, the daffodils were browning and dying off but the apple blossoms and cherry blossoms were taking all the glory.

"Look, William," and with as much dignity as I could gather in my skirts, I threw myself up into the cherry tree I knew I could climb.

William laughed and picked a taller tree to climb. He was not hampered by skirts or short legs; he made it look effortless.

I heard a cough that I recognised.

"That's Dad," I whispered to William. If he found me in here on my own with William, it might make him as angry as he had been with Ceinwen for walking out with Rhodri. I froze and put my fingers on my lips to silence William.

Dad's dark figure plodded past the orchard door. He should have been at work in the quarry. What was wrong? Bees, cherry trees, gold and sheep lost their appeal suddenly. I slipped down and went to the door in the wall. William was behind me. We could see Dad up at the farmhouse scraping his boots by the kitchen door. I waited until he had gone in, to visit the Gruffudds, then said goodbye to William and went back down the track.

When I got home, Mam said she did not know where Dad was. She thought he was at the quarry. But, she said, she was worried about him. His cough was getting worse.

Chapter Eight

The chapel thronged with people, silent, respectfully listening, with their coats on to keep warm. There were rich deep voices, light clear voices, gruff and husky voices almost singing out the words from the Bible. Some spoke quietly, some gently, some barely audible, some were lively, some were rousing, some were brilliant. Everyone entered in with great aplomb sharing nerves, applause and smirks. The night had been crisp and clear and we had all congregated at the chapel next to the schoolroom. The lamps scented the room with a close cosy paraffin aroma. Almost everyone from the village was there.

From the moment blind Jacob plucked the first note on his harp as a musical interlude, up until when my name was called out, my mouth went dry, my hands clammy and my feet felt heavy. But when I stood and looked out across the pews of people the words came. I remembered them all. They danced across the upturned faces of every listener.

"Let the redeemed of the Lord *tell their story—" (Psalm 107:2)*

I let my pauses breathe.

"Some wandered in desert wastelands finding no way to a city where they could settle." (Psalm 107.4)

My voice rose.

"Let them give thanks to the Lord *for his unfailing love, and his*

wonderful deeds for mankind, for he satisfies the thirsty and fills the hungry with good things." (Psalm 107:8–9)

My voice lowered and I spoke slowly.

"Some became fools through their rebellious ways and suffered affliction because of their iniquities." (Psalm 107:17)

I let the words judge my listeners and prick their conscience with careful enunciation.

"Some went out on the sea in ships; they were merchants on the mighty waters. They saw the works of the LORD, his wonderful deeds in the deep. For he spoke and stirred up a tempest that lifted high the waves. They mounted up to the heavens and went down to the depths; in their peril their courage melted away. They reeled and staggered like drunkards; they were at their wits' end." (Psalm 107:23–27)

I made it uplifting with dramatic inflection.

"Then they cried out to the LORD in their trouble, and he brought them out of their distress. He stilled the storm to a whisper; the waves of the sea were hushed. They were glad when it grew calm, and he guided them to their desired haven." (Psalm 107:28–30)

I reminded them with joy, to hope and be thankful.

"Let them give thanks to the LORD for his unfailing love and his wonderful deeds for mankind. Let them exalt him in the assembly of the people and praise him in the council of the elders." (Psalm 107:31–32)

Mam, Dad and Ifan watched me. Dad coughed his way through the entire evening and interjected the silences with his familiar, dry "peswch".

As competitors, we sat in the same pew all together. Ioan Thomas, Gareth's brother, sat next to me. He was the youngest and gave a convincing recitation that put him on the probable winner list. The judges, from Trem y Mynydd, sat on the other side of the aisle.

However, there was one competitor who was outstanding. She turned the words into music and the Bible into poetry. Her voice was rich and clear, and her pauses and inflection were perfect. Non won—the right decision. Miss Evans would be pleased that a girl had taken the trophy. Mr Price, as minister, would be pleased it was one of his pupils. It was fitting for Bible recitation and for all the extra tuition he had given her. The judges made kind comments about the rest of us and one spoke to me afterwards saying how well they thought I had presented my psalm. I was disappointed I hadn't won.

When all was said and done, we mingled in the murmur of relaxed conversation. I saw William across the room, talking with my cousin Owen. William was drawing something on his palm with his forefinger. Owen listened, nodding in agreement with his arms folded and his finger on his chin. I made my way towards them. The tall figure of Mr Price, Gweinidog stood over me. His face was in shadow. Non was beside him. The light reflected off her cheeks and she beamed.

"*Llongyfarchiadau*, Non," I said.

"*Diolch*," she smiled.

"Elin," Mr Price acknowledged me. "You did well."

"Thank you." I couldn't see his smile.

"But Non was outstanding." He was parading her like a trophy. I nodded and, not knowing what else to say, excused myself.

Before I reached William, Ifan caught my hand.

"Well done, Elin," he said. "I thought you were the best."

"No, Non was definitely the winner. It has been a long time since a girl has won. Ifan, did you see Ceinwen?"

Ceinwen had come in and stood in the dusky light at the back of the chapel just as I began my recitation. A redheaded lad, the same one she had introduced me to at chapel who led them in song as they walked, had stood with her. It occurred to me that she might be walking out with him. But by the time the judges had announced their decision and Non had been awarded a book as a prize, I looked to the back and Ceinwen and the redhead had gone. I could not see them anywhere.

Ifan was shaking his head.

"Did she come?"

I explained.

"I guess she didn't want to cross Dad's path in case he got angry, but he hasn't been drinking." He shook his head. "Ah well. Elin, I haven't had a chance to tell you yet."

Ifan had changed the conversation before I said anything more about Ceinwen.

"Mam mentioned the other day that she'd like to go and see Llinos only she hasn't the time. I suggested you might go instead, and go by yourself. You're getting taller by the day, Elin. It must be Mam's *lobsgóws*," he laughed.

"Thank you!" I kissed Ifan on the cheek. To him, I would always be a baby sister no matter how old I was. He had kindly remembered our conversation about Llinos and had taken all the effort out of me asking Mam. As for Ceinwen's disappearance, if she was walking out with the redhead she may well not want Dad to know in case he "spoiled everything".

I saw William out of the corner of my eye, looking at us. He came across the room.

"Well done, Elin. You chose a wonderful Psalm." Ifan

dissolved away to talk to Owen and William bent close.

"I have something to tell you." His eyes gleamed.

"Real gold?" I asked.

"Mmm, unless you're a fool," he teased, not giving anything away and before he could properly answer, Mam swept by and caught me.

"It's time to go, Elin," she fussed.

I looked at William. "What?" I mouthed but couldn't read the answer in his eyes. He just grinned at me. Mam was very insistent, and as Dad materialised beside us, shortly followed by Ifan, I pulled a sorry face at William. We left.

It was a week after the recitation that I had the chance to go across the scrubby heathland and down to the cliff top where Llinos lived, at the foot of Moel Gras. The week had been a busy one. Mam had taken it into her head to spring clean and she had involved me with lots of chores. Now, at last, I had some time to see Llinos. It was a Wednesday with a half day at school, and Mam had no chores for me. The weather was getting warmer and the days longer. She sent me with some bread and vegetables for Llinos and *bara brith* for Ceinwen. I had never been to see Llinos on my own before, and though I knew the way well from having gone with Mam, I needed clear instructions from there to Plas Horon. It was very grown up.

Llinos kept a cottage in a sorry state by the cliffs. She collected cockles, mussels and laverbread for market, standing in the sands of the straits with her undignified skirts tucked up, scouring and searching. She balanced her basket on her head. Enduring the cold for hours at a time, she was as unkempt as the heather and her moods were as wild as the turns of the tide. Rumours ran from her cottage and kept strangers away, so few visited ever, though she would take her wares from door to door to sell after she had boiled them in her cauldron. And Betsi, the cockle seller, would come and buy her cockles from her and take them to market. In the autumn and winter, my sister would explore the estuary for mussels.

I opened the door with a loud knock. Llinos was shocked but her fierce features faded when she saw it was me. She swished around poking the grate and putting the kettle on the range.

"Elin, Elin, Elin," she sang. "Am I glad to see you—and look at you, like a reed."

She twittered on chirpily and sat me down while she made some tea.

Suddenly she put her face close to mine and peered intently at me. I laughed. She didn't. She ran her finger tenderly along the scar across my eye.

"It has faded a little," she said.

It had not faded at all. I was always likened in looks to Llinos until that fateful day when I had disfigured my face. I was helping Uncle John up at the farm. It was early June and we were bringing in the hay. I tripped on a stook and fell onto the seat of his new hay tedder that he had brought to the farm at vast expense. Metal cut across my eyebrow and cheek and opened a deep gash. It took a long time to heal. Mam went to Mam Meredith up on the edge of Trem y Mynydd for ointment but, I was ashamed, it made little difference. I would always have a white scar instead of an eyebrow although I might look less permanently startled, if the hair would only grow again.

I looked at Llinos. She had become a little disfigured

too. You would never know now that she was once talked about for her radiant velvet skin and black silk hair. Today her skin was creased and crumpled. Her features sagged and fell, while her hair straggled raggedly in salt and pepper twists.

"Mam sent these for you."

I gave her the basket. Our visits were never made with empty hands. Mam had first brought me to see Llinos when I was tiny and Llinos was just married. Jonny was often away for long periods of time and it was always then that we would come to see her, when she was on her own. We brought her treats from our garden. I could not really remember Jonny except from their wedding day, smiling by her side.

A single apple tree outside her cottage told the tale of the seasons that passed. I would climb that one too whenever we came to see her, leaves on, leaves off, when it was in blossom and when I could pick the russet apples from it. It was a gnarled little tree. I was too big for it now.

Llinos had a baby, a beautiful black-haired baby boy. And then came that horrible day when we found her rotting in degradation. We hadn't been to see her for a while and we found her all alone. No Jonathan. No *baban*. Old wives whispered that the sea claimed its own, that Jonny lay in a watery grave, but of the baby no one knew. Llinos would not say. She lost her dignity, her name of wife and mother, her mind and her spirit snapped like a twig across life's knee. Mam would not tell me what had happened. I was too much a child to understand.

Despite the sadness, Llinos had moments of clarity that were insightful. She had gathered and buried jewels of wisdom along her troubled path, and it was these that

I came to find today. Like Uncle John, you could talk to Llinos with no risk of judgement, and she would read in between the words and seemingly understand. She would not give you any advice unless you asked. Sometimes she talked nonsense, but that did not matter because she listened. My secret sister was great treasure to me.

I talked and talked and talked as I could to no other. I told her of the rumours about Ceinwen and Rhodri. I told her about Dad's anger and drunkenness that was so predictable yet unpredictable. I told her how William thought he had found gold and how I thought it was fool's gold. I told her about the chapel in Trem y Mynydd where I had sat through a service, beside Uncle John.

She just listened and twittered occasionally. Then she got up and offered me some breakfast, bacon and laverbread. It was the afternoon, but I accepted. Delicious! A strong flavour of the sea, fried in oatmeal and bacon fat, was washed down with tea. I was ravenous.

While we ate she talked and I listened.

"Wealth gained quickly will dwindle away, but those who gather it little by little will become rich," she started out by saying. "Little by little," she repeated. To gather wealth a bit at a time I thought sounded wise. Llinos knew how to gather little by little in the estuary with her rake through the sand. I tucked her words into a pocket in my mind. Then she talked about gathering mussels, rich pearls in the cold, cold waters. When she didn't make sense and started crying, she began to scare me.

"Llinos?" I asked her. "Why are you crying?"

With a desolate look, she turned to me and asked,

"Why did they take Jonny from me? Why did he go with them?"

"No one took Jonny, Llinos. You know that."

At least, no one had taken him in the little bit of the story I had been told. The haunting look on her face made it all too plain that Llinos was lost. She was in a lonely place and the truth distorted in her mind. The story I had been told was that Jonny's boat had never returned on the night of the *storom fawr*. His brother had been with him. Neither of them had ever been found, no bodies, no boat. It was the story all the fishermen's wives lived in shadowy fear of. Poor Llinos! Jonny was lost at sea, no longer a fisherman, but fish food. A shiver went down my spine. I did not want to think about it.

And then, snap! With a click of the fingers, she began speaking clearly as if there had been no tears, telling me that William had found gold and that it would not be easily gained wealth. He would need to work hard to get it but that it would be good. She seemed excited. It was like she was foretelling the future. I was confused. So I stood behind her chair and put my arms around her. I told her that I loved her. She gently tugged my pained wrist and rested her head against my shoulder. Quiet for a while, we nested in a contented, sisterly *cwtsh*.

"You are always welcome here, Elin," she said. "You know that, don't you? You're a big girl now. You'll come and see me again, won't you?"

I left her then and climbed Moel Gras, the mountain that rose up from the flat plains behind Llinos' cottage, following the instructions Mam had given me. It was exciting to be running errands far from home, on my own. Tufted dry grass guarded the iron brown spring and dark green reeds flagged the marshy patches. I chose my way carefully so my feet did not sink or my boots get wet.

The incline levelled out near the top making it easier. The ground was firmer here. Wild ponies and sheep had made short work of the grass. Moel Gras was a different sort of mountain, softer and more rounded. It was all grass. There were no stones exposed, like on Carreg Du.

On the top, I stood and looked around a full circle. I could see the glint of the Straits between *Ynys Môn* and Caernarfon where buildings sat like people picnicking on the shores beside the castle, a big grey rock. I could see Carreg Du, the proud protector of our valley and I could see the fertile flatter lands inland to which I was heading. Plas Horon was hidden by woodland after windless fields. Some were ploughed still and empty. Others were full of grazing grasses and sheep or cows. The trees, around their perimeters, were a mottled tapestry of blossoms, light browns and greens where the new leaves were breaking through.

Looking back out to sea, that crystal sea, Llinos' cottage was a tiny dot, all alone, the apple tree just visible. Poor Llinos! She was like an earthenware pot that had been painted and made to look beautiful. Life had picked her up, thrown her into turmoil and shattered her into a thousand pieces that others tried to stick back together again, but she was never the same. She could not contain anything in her pot except a few shrouded secrets. Was there any hope for her? I recalled that haunting look. How often was she lost and trapped by her fears?

What though clouds are hovering o'er me
And I seem to walk alone

Those words to that hymn Uncle John had been singing

in the chapel came to me. How apt!

> *Longing 'mid my cares and crosses*
> *For the joys that now have flown*

They were playing in my head. I could hear Uncle John singing them.

> *If I've Jesus, "Jesus only,"*
> *Then my sky will have a gem;*
> *He's the sun of brightest splendour*
> *And the star of Bethlehem*

I looked up at the plumage of feathery fluff that pillowed in the sky and with them the words vapourised and blew across my mind.

> *What though clouds are hovering o'er me*
> *And I seem to walk alone—*
> *Longing 'mid my cares and crosses*
> *For the joys that now have flown*

Llinos walked alone. Her joys had flown. That was true. Clouds of confusion seemed to hover over her. What was she longing for? I was glad I had seen her. I felt brighter for having talked to her today.

…my sky will have a gem…if I've Jesus.

Pulling myself together into my shawl, I turned to head inland. My knees took the strain of climbing down and I went fast. I jumped the tufts and almost ran. By the time I reached the level fields I felt refreshed and washed in the new life spring brings. The bees were busy in the bright splendour of the sweet-smelling gorse. A swallow flipped and twisted in front of me as an arrow pointing the way to summer coming. It dipped to catch a gnat along the way. It was warmer here away from the sea breeze and I shed my shawl, draping it over my arm. The birds were rustling their nests together with song. An angry blackbird shouted at me for coming too close to his missus, and a thrush spat a beak-full of moss at me in shock as it almost flew into me.

Through the woods a narrow path led with the musty rotted remnants of autumn, now dried out, littering the way beside bluebells that splattered colour on the carpet and spilled over the edge of the deep ancient ditch. I climbed down into the sheltered dingle that guided my route to the bridge and followed the track out of the trees. There I met the main Caernarfon road by the farm. A dog barked a warning to me and a black and red coach went past with the horses straining forward. I followed in its wake.

The coach turned in at the great gates to Plas Horon. I could see the stone lions that guarded the arch. They disregarded me as I passed—their look aloof and disdainful. I was too small in stature to compare to the usual grandeur that passed beneath their portal, too lowly. I walked on until I reached the saw mill on the river's edge. Here a path went around the engineer's house to the back of the main house. Ceinwen had described it all in anxious detail after she first came to find work. There was no doubt this was the right way.

It felt as if the sun had induced an afternoon slumber on the countryside, but around the corner was a courtyard of activity. There were people scuttling at their antics, up and down steps outside the buildings and beavering with laden arms across the stone cobbles. I was about to ask directions to the laundry when I saw Ceinwen walk out with a great white sheet and shake it in the courtyard. Another girl came forward, took a corner and together they straightened and folded it. I dashed across the cobbles and surprised Ceinwen by handing her the *bara brith* I had brought from Mam.

"Are you all on your own, Elin?"

She sent the white sheet in with her companion saying she only had a minute to share. In the light, she looked so clean and fresh. She wanted to know how everyone was. I gave her all the news I could think of. Then I remembered.

"I saw you at the recitation." She smiled. "I came to hear you, Elin. You made me proud."

"Why didn't you stay until the end?"

"I was on my way to a prayer meeting. I had hoped I might catch you speaking so I took a detour on the way to Trem y Mynydd and Huw insisted on coming with me. You did well."

She rested her hand on my shoulder.

"Now tell me, how is Dad?"

I briefly shared Ifan's story of Dad's sorry state after she left on Mothering Sunday, and concluded, "Dad doesn't seem well."

"What's the matter?"

"I don't know. He has a constant cough and has been drinking more."

"And how is Llinos?" she asked. I told her of my visit to the cliff tops.

"I know it is hard to see her struggle. It breaks my heart too," Ceinwen responded. "It was good that you went to see her. I'll go and visit her soon, too. She needs healing. There is hope."

I stared at her blankly.

"What does that mean?"

"Elin, I wish I had the time to tell you everything, but I must get back to work now. I want to tell you what has happened and how I have met Jesus since I have been going to the chapel in Trem y Mynydd. Come and see me again, *cariad*. I'll tell you everything. Or come to chapel with Uncle John."

Met Jesus?

She kissed my scar.

"Now, I must go!"

I went home a different way. I followed the track that Ceinwen and her companions took every Sunday to Trem y Mynydd. Then I cut down into the valley, above where William and I explored. I could see the *nant*.

Half the valley was already in shadow. The stream was a thinner trickle of water than the frothing flush into which William had thrust his basket. This was the *nant* in a spring mood—not in good humour. It was almost running dry in a lazy way.

I stopped.

There was a man standing in the *nant*. He was standing roughly where William had been the day he showed me the gold. His black back faced me, so I crouched beside a boulder in case he should turn. He did not move and nor did I. Only the water ran over his hand in perpetual motion. He wore a black hat. I waited.

A seagull flew overhead, casting a shadow that glided across the sunlit flanks of the mountain on the other side. I watched it, craning my neck, and saw another figure coming down into the valley. In sunshine, this new visitor was unaware of us and was coming at a nonchalant pace, ambling his way over the rocks, stopping now and again to look at his feet. He was wearing a brown, wool jacket and a flat cap. The sun lit the back of his head as he bent down. It was William. He straightened, scanned the valley and froze. He had seen the man too.

He stepped forward like a prey animal, mindful of its predator, and paused by a big rock. A crunch, a slip, a slither of small stones and he advanced. He hesitated and stopped again, resting his hand on the wooden box slung on his hip.

The man straightened up, tall and slim. I still could not see his face. William came head to head with him on the slope of rock and together they spoke for a long time. Was this an arranged meeting? I couldn't tell. William opened the box on his hip and lifted out a white ferret, holding it firmly beneath its front legs. It hung in his hand like a stocky walking stick, tail straight down and back legs splayed out. Then he put it back.

In exchange, the man held his hand out, with his palm to the sky and they both peered intently at it as if their future depended on it. The man put the contents in his pocket, touched his hat and began climbing the way William had just descended. William stood looking at the swirls and bluffs of the stream. He stood there a long time. A cloud came over the sun, darkening the whole valley before William began making his way home by the route we had first taken together. The black figure had disappeared.

I crept out from behind my boulder, and by the time I had climbed the ridge, William was nowhere to be seen.

When I reached the farm, Owen came out of the kitchen door and nearly walked into me.

"Elin!" He looked surprised. "Have you come for your Dad?"

"No. Why?"

"He's here. I think the sun has got to him, or something. He's not making much sense. He keeps talking about blasting rocks."

I went in to the cool kitchen and Mrs Gruffudd was standing with an enamel cup of water in her hand.

"Ah Elin."

Dad was sat at the table. He looked tired. Uncle John sat opposite. They both looked at me bewildered.

"Help me walk your Dad home," Uncle John said, pushing his chair back from the table. Dad rose up unsteadily. I held his arm. He was drunk again.

Chapter Nine

Mam shouted at Dad. He had spent a lot of money on drink and she was cross because he wouldn't tell her where the money came from. He was not fit for work. There was no way he could be suspended by a rope while drumming a jumper into the rock face, safely, in the state he was in. Ifan had gone to work without him. Dad was getting worse—I was sure of it—and Mam did not know what to do.

After school, I went up to the farm to escape facing either of them. There was no one around, so I climbed the cherry tree in the orchard and leant back against the trunk. I could see the village, the sea and the quarry. The hum of the quarry drifted across the bracken-side towards me. It had been a noisy morning with lots of blasts that made the ground shake. The giant's steps were being carved higher up the mountainside. Trwyn Glas had changed shape a few times in my life.

From where I sat I could not see the quay, but the boat was in. Its stern was just visible beneath the reflective sheen of the slate cottage roofs. The bees droned. The cherry blossoms nodded. It was warm. Drowsiness crept over me like a sea mist. I would have fallen asleep, but the trunk of the tree was narrow and dug into my back. Up the track came a horse and cart laden with barrels. It was

William. I waved and jumped down. He didn't see me until I reached the door in the wall. He stalled Blodyn for a minute and I climbed up beside him.

"Where's Uncle John?" I asked.

"He went to see your Mam. How is your Dad?"

I was embarrassed. Was it common knowledge that Dad was not good?

"Oh! He's fine." I lied.

I looked at the barrels in the back of the cart.

"*Ga i dy helpu?*"

"If you want to." The idea amused him. "I'd be glad of some help," he said.

We pulled into the courtyard of the farm and William backed Blodyn between the barns.

"So?" I had to know. "What was it you wanted to tell me the other evening at the recitation? Have you found any more gold?"

He shook his head keeping his eyes on Blodyn.

"No. I found something else."

"In the valley?" Perhaps that meeting with the man had been arranged.

"Something more precious than gold." He smiled. "I found it a few weeks ago." What could be more precious than gold?

"You were there too," he said, without looking at me.

"*Naddo?* You didn't see me, did you?"

"Yes, before you left."

I thought I had hidden myself well behind the rock.

"Oh! I didn't think anyone saw me," I said. "I thought I had stayed hidden until you'd gone."

"Pardon?" His eyes were dancing like the sunlight

glistening on the blue sea.

"I saw you with Ceinwen at the end of the service. But you had disappeared before I could get to you."

I chuckled. What a misunderstanding!

"Did you enjoy it?"

What? That chapel service with Uncle John when William had made a fool of himself and told everyone he was a sinner. He saw the uncertain shadows shift across my face, but the amusement did not leave his.

"I don't understand, William," I said. "You're not a sinner. Of all the people I know— "

He had climbed down and secured Blodyn's reins. Being all gentlemanly to me suddenly, he came round and held out his hand to help me down.

"All have sinned and fall short, child." He teased in a preacher voice. "Mind you don't trip." I jumped from the footplate. I was no lady.

"Yes, but you aren't bad."

"It isn't like that, Elin." He was serious. "It's not about whether we are bad or not. Everybody does things wrong at times. Don't tell me you have never told a lie. You have, haven't you? If you tell me you have never told a lie, I'll know you're lying." He laughed but spoke sincerely. "I am a sinner," he said. "I have done lots of things I am ashamed of."

Me too, when he put it like that. I could think of plenty of times I had felt shame.

"I have done lots of things that have made God sad."

God sad?

He hurried on before I could interrupt. "It was when I saw Jesus that everything changed."

Saw Jesus?

"What do you mean *saw* Jesus?"

He sounded like Ceinwen. "Met Jesus," she had said. She had met Jesus at chapel. I frowned. Imagine walking up to Jesus in the chapel and shaking hands with him: "Hello Jesus, nice to meet you!"

William continued talking while we put all the barrels of lime in their place in the barn.

"I wanted to tell you all about it at the recitation, but your Mam took you away." He pretended to look sad and I felt less awkward.

"Didn't Non do well?"

His head went down and he rolled another barrel into place. The lime would be used for a variety of things, from whitewashing the walls and fighting potato blight to fertilising the fields; it was a farmer's friend, and Uncle John kept himself well stocked.

"What did you mean when you said you had found something more precious than gold?" I asked.

"That's just it," he said. "That's what I'd hoped to explain to you. When I confessed that I was a sinner, that evening, I saw Jesus. He took everything I ever did, that made God sad, away. He took everything that I was ever ashamed of. Gone. Forgotten. Thrown into the sea. Never to be remembered again." William gestured to illustrate his point. "And it was just him and me, face to face. I saw him and saw that he doesn't judge me. He accepts me just as I am. He is like gold but more exciting, more amazing, more valuable. I want to live my life for him and with him, doing what he wants me to do, not what I want to do. I know he's with me. He speaks to me and I can hear him."

William was excited. "I go to the chapel in Trem y Mynydd now every week, and every prayer meeting. It's amazing. God is doing something wonderful. I could never have imagined I would see such changes in people. Last week, a lady came from Pen y Bont. She was deaf but the minister prayed for her and she could hear."

We kept rolling and stacking the barrels, side by side. I let his words sink in. It did sound amazing. Certainly something had happened to William. I had noticed something different about Ceinwen too, when I went with her to the chapel. It was hard to believe that William was even more excited about Jesus than mining ventures.

"So does that mean you will forget about the gold?"

"No! I can't. But I must put Jesus first in everything. He comes first. I believe he will help me."

We carried on in silence.

"And what did you mean, when you said you stayed hidden from me?"

It was his turn to ask me a question.

"What were you talking about?"

We had finished. William leant back against one of the barrels with his arms and legs crossed, his head tilted.

"The other day, when you were out ferreting above the *nant*," I said, "I saw you come down into the valley and there was a man there by the water."

Instantly the glint of laughter was gone from his eyes. He stared at me levelly for a minute then his shoulders drooped and he considered the dust on his clog-soled boots. He did not speak and the silence grew dark.

"Yes," he said, eventually. "I don't know what to do, Elin."

"Well, why don't you ask Jesus?" I was being facetious.

William grinned. "I have done, but I still don't have answers."

"So, who was that man?" I asked.

"Mr Price, Gweinidog."

"Mr Price?" I remembered it was Mr Price who had found fool's gold in the mountains.

"He showed me some quartz he had found. *Tyrd*! We can't stand around doing nothing."

I followed him out of the barn, helped take Blodyn out of the cart and remove her tack. I took her harness into the little stone room beside the barn, while William put her in the paddock. We sat with the harness on our laps and talked as we cleaned each part. Mr Price, Gweinidog seemed to know about stones. He knew the difference between fool's gold and real gold and therefore might know something about mining. He might be able to help.

"Did you not agree to meet him there?" I asked.

William reacted like I had slapped him with a stinging nettle.

"No!" He said, "I think Mr Price is looking for gold, too. He had a handful of minerals he had found in the *nant*. Thankfully, none of them were gold he showed me, but I don't trust him."

"Was any of it fool's gold?"

"No."

"Do you know the difference between fool's gold and real gold?"

"It's a gut feeling, Elin. I am sure I have found gold and Mr Price is looking for it too."

"What if he finds some? He will know sooner than you

whether it is fool's gold or not."

"That's what worries me."

"William, I know you hope to one day have a mine, but you're just a boy. It's impossible. You can't build a mine now, can you?"

"A boy with dreams and Jesus to guide me!" The glint returned in his eye. "They are big dreams, Elin, but not impossible."

I laughed. "But surely Mr Price has Jesus to guide him too? He's a minister, *y gweinidog*. If he finds gold in that valley, he is someone who can get all he needs. People will listen to him and do what he says. People won't believe you if you tell them you have found gold, but they'll believe him right away."

William shrugged. "Everyone can have Jesus to guide them if they choose to listen to him, but not everyone does."

That picture, called *"Gweddi"*, of the devil on the old lady's shawl in chapel and Ifan telling me that even the devil can go to chapel with the religious came to mind.

"I will listen to Jesus first and do what he tells me. Joshua made his army march around Jericho for seven days. That made no sense, but he won the battle by doing it God's way."

I was not convinced. William carried on talking and described in detail the rainbow rock in his valley of gold. He said that on the edge of a boulder by the scree, a stone's throw from the *nant*, he had found black slate with white quartz and what, he felt sure, was a skein of glistening pink gold. It was a very fine line. He described something different from the particles of fool's gold I had seen on Mr Price's desk and from the granite in the quarry.

"It must be worth something. Got to be! There might not be enough to make bullion, but what is there must be worth something."

"You need to find someone who would know."

The idea that Mr Price might find it too hung over us threateningly. I remembered I had once heard Uncle John and Owen talking about the mines down near Barmouth. I suggested he should talk to them. Maybe they would know someone? And to whom did the land belong anyhow? There were so many questions. How did you start a mine, anyway?

I re-buckled the piece of harness I had been cleaning and, standing, handed it to William to put away. We were done.

"Shall we get some rabbits?"

I waited while William got his ferrets and nets, and then we clambered up through the woods to the outer edge. William kept on about mine prospects.

"Just imagine it," he said. "It would bring jobs. There would be more work for people like your Dad and Ifan."

I wasn't convinced Dad was doing very well with the job he had.

"And just imagine if Mr Price, Gweinidog found your skein of gold and managed to start a mine first," I said.

"I will pray that he doesn't."

We caught a number of baby rabbits and William, holding them by their back legs, handed me three to take to Mam. There wasn't much meat, but it would be succulent. We headed directly back through the woods towards the village. When we got to the edge by the road that led into Nant and were still amongst the trees I stopped to tighten my bootlace. Suddenly, William signalled to me not to move. I stood up. He was peering down from the embankment onto the road. I crept up to his shoulder.

"What is it?" I whispered.

Beneath us, on the road, were two men, one in black, his face hidden by his trilby. As we watched, he handed a package to the man opposite him, in quarryman's garb and a flat cap who stood square, facing us clearly.

"Dad?"

"Shh!" William hushed me and tried to shuffle me back out of sight in the trees.

"Come on," he said once we were hidden again.

"But I want to see," I protested. "What's Dad doing? Who's he talking to?"

"Come on," he repeated.

"William!" He vexed me.

Without a word he took me home.

Mam was sitting with a rag-rug across her lap. The sacking, without any rags attached, fanned out towards the range. She looked up with her hook in her hand as I came in. I hung the rabbits in the scullery.

"Where's Dad?" I asked.

"On a late shift."

I raised my eyebrows.

"He was well enough to go."

"How is Uncle John?"

"*Iawn*," she replied. "He had news."

"Oh?" I enquired sitting on the settle sideways and tucking my feet up beneath my skirts.

"Er—boots!" Mam reminded me.

"Yes."

She pulled a loop of cloth through the sacking before continuing.

"Owen is going to marry."

"That's exciting." I felt pleased for him. He had only recently started courting Tanwen, Mared's youngest sister.

"They will wait a bit. He will build her a cottage first," Mam said.

Tanwen was the same age as Ceinwen and Ifan.

Uncle John had come up, today, to see how Dad was and to ask for Ifan and Dad's help, if Dad was well enough. He wasn't ill. I had just seen him halfway up the hill out of the valley. He looked fine. He just drank too much.

Owen—getting married; my imagination came alive and I could see Tanwen sitting by the window of a sweet, grey-stone cottage with red window frames and lintels, newly built in the bottom pasture. She would be sitting there making lace and looking out to sea while Owen was outside turning the hay—quiet, dependable Owen, who said little but felt deep and was as steady and encouraging as Uncle John.

"Tanwen said Mared's not well."

Mam casually brought me back to reality. Mared was my brother Dewi's wife.

"Is it the baby?" I asked.

"I don't know. Elin, come with me on Saturday. I want to help. We'll set off early in the morning and go and see them." This reminded me.

"Mam, I've hung some rabbits in the back for you."

Ifan returned in time for tea. Dad came in a little late. He was gruff and tired.

"Did you see him, Dad?" Ifan asked as soon as he came in and I pricked up my ears.

"Who?" asked Mam.

"Jabez Price. He wanted to see me. I met him, today, on the way to Trem y Mynydd."

I thought Dad was on the late shift. What was he doing going to Trem y Mynydd? I had never heard Mr Price, Gweinidog called Jabez before, but as soon as Dad said it, I realised how familiar that figure was, and in my mind I saw him in the valley talking to William.

"You never said." Mam sounded cross.

"He remembers me, Annie. He remembers me from when I worked down south. "

"Dad worked down south?" I asked.

"Only for a couple of years, in a coal mine, while there was no work here. It was before I met your Mam. Jabez Price was a boy in Brynamman."

Chapter Ten

That was the summer my freedom came to an end. As the days lengthened and warmed, Owen's prediction that Mam would be sending me out to work appeared on the horizon sooner than I'd thought. It all began in a simple way, when I went to help our family.

We set out early, as the sun woke one Saturday, both with baskets full of Mam's baking and Mrs Gruffudd's kindness.

"I can't wait to see those little ones." Mam cheerfully began, but by the time we reached the track to Trem y Mynydd, I realised her joints were aching.

"Why didn't you ask Uncle John if we could take the cart?"

We weren't far from home and still had miles to reach Bethesda.

"I didn't want to trouble him," she said.

"I could go and get it," I suggested.

"Besides I thought they would need it. Dad and Ifan are going to help gather stones for the cottage, today."

"Oh? Where from?" I asked.

"In the valleys above the farm; your Dad said there are some good rocks up there."

"They won't get a cart up there." I stopped to look down at the sort of terrain they would be dealing with.

"Wait here, Mam, and I'll run down to the farm and ask if we can take the cart."

"No, Elin. I'll be fine," she assured me. "Come on. They will need it."

If they would be looking for rocks in William's valley of gold, perhaps William would speak to Owen about the gold mines in Barmouth. The last time I had seen William he had been dripping in oil from shearing the sheep. He was sweaty and greasy with his shirt sleeves rolled up.

The sun had reached its full height by the time we arrived in Bethesda, and Mam's temper was brittle and dry. She was in pain, but as soon as she saw Arwel and Abner standing barefoot in the doorway of Dewi's home, she revived. The boys stared at us, empty-eyed.

"Arwel! Abner!" She kissed their cheeks. "Is your Mam here?"

They looked so listless. Abner let go of the doorpost. His small hand signalled to us to go inside. Arwel shyly sidestepped me. I smiled at him but the expression in his big eyes did not change. They were wide and staring out of hollow cheeks. Mam pushed the door fully open and the sunlight fell from dusty windows where a small placard read *"Nid oes BRADWR yn y ty hwn"*—*"There is not a Traitor in this house"*—above the lace curtain.

"Dewi?" Mam asked anxiously as she went in.

It took a minute for my eyes to adjust to the dark interior and when they did, I could see Dewi sitting dejected by the range with Tomos on his lap.

"Mam?" He had raised his head in surprise and slowly stood up. She put her basket on the bare table by the window.

"How is Mared?" Her crisp words were full of concern.

He shook his head at her while I squinted to study his empty expression.

"She's asleep," he said. Mam bustled into action but stopped when she saw the fire was out.

"No coal."

She was angry then. She reached out and grabbed the back of the placard in the window, pulled it down and ripped it into small pieces, scattering them in the ash in the range.

"I don't know why you still have that. What good did it do you anyway? And when the agreement was made, what then? Nothing's changed has it?"

"*Na.*" Dewi's head sadly swung from side to side.

Dewi was no traitor, no Judas. He had remained loyal to the workers throughout the lockout. But it had brought them naught. The lockout had forced the quarrymen to down their tools. Instead the dispute brought division to their community. The traitors all congregated in the fancy church. The loyal men stayed in the chapels and sung in choirs to raise money for those who needed it most. Still Penrhyn lorded it over them in his gothic castle on the coast, and conditions and pay were no better. In bitterness men were walking away to find pride in work elsewhere.

"Come and work with Dad." Mam said. Dewi considered in silence—a long silence. The air had become dark and thick with implication. It was like Mam and Dewi were stirring a stodgy pottage of thoughts around and around. I think Dewi had been sitting there stirring that pottage of thoughts for many days, without any coal to warm him.

"But what about Ifan?" I interrupted.

If Dewi came to work with Dad the pay would have to be shared. Men worked together in family groups and would haggle with the managers for a fair price for their rock, for their bargain. Mind you, the way Dad was these days that might be a good thing. Maybe Dad would welcome Dewi's help?

"It is better to have a little than nothing. We can manage." Mam replied with certainty. She had made up her mind, but Dewi protested.

"I can't leave Mared and the boys," he said.

"What if Elin stayed here to look after them?" Mam suggested.

Mam shuffled her hand in her basket and gave the boys each one of Mrs Gruffudd's loft-room apples. She also pulled out a black and red jar, scuttled into the scullery and came back with an enamel mug. We all stood staring blankly as she disappeared out of the door. The boys stayed, expressionless and motionless with the apples in their hands. No one spoke.

Mam came back. She had pilfered hot water from a neighbour's kettle. Upstairs she went with a mug of beef tea for Mared; Dewi relaxed. He sat back down with Tomos, who squirmed in his arms. When he set him down on the floor Tomos crawled across to my skirts and I lifted him up. He grabbed my plaits and tugged them.

"Ouch!" I tickled his tummy and he giggled.

And so, I came to stay in Bethesda doing the work of a woman, looking after my nephews. With Mam's interference things turned around. Mared grew stronger and more rounded. Dewi not worrying over her was a relief too. Although, I struggled to understand how my inexperienced efforts at keeping a home could have relieved her.

Every week, my mother came and brought a sheep's head from Mrs Gruffudd and enough coal to warm the *lobsgóws*. Sometimes Mrs Gruffudd came too, in the trap, to take the weight off Mam's weary limbs. One day, *Y Parchedig* from one of the chapels came to visit, the Reverend Job. He didn't bring any food or money, but he did pray with Mared. He had lost both his wife and his daughters, who died within three years of each other and understood grief, though he never mentioned it. He talked solely about God and his goodness. Reverend Job came into the cottage like the first morning rays of sunshine on the horizon and brought hope.

I tried my best to improve things too, and I made sure there was less dust in that little cottage than when I first came. At night, I crawled between the sheets I had washed, dried and ironed, more tired than I had ever known. Mared instructed me from her bed when I didn't know what to do. She soon became strong enough to get up and come and sit by the back door, mending and making garments for the new baby.

There she sat and sang. It was beautiful. The Reverend Job heard her and said she had a gift. He invited her to chapel and, one evening, she went. When she came home later, she was glowing, saying she had been cleansed, washed in the blood. That sounded messy to me, and I thought the prospect of giving birth was muddling her head, but Mared began to attend chapel regularly. She had been redeemed by her Saviour, she said.

I worked hard and thought of William, remembering him delivering a lamb. He was gentle with the ewe. I thought of him sewing jackets on the orphaned lambs. He wanted them to survive and was kind in giving them a good chance. He made an excellent shepherd, but if he had a choice he would choose to mine. He was more adventurous.

I was experiencing the work that women took great pride in and girls left school for. Although it was satisfying, I didn't like the feeling that I had not chosen it. I wondered what it was like to work in a gold mine. Could girls work in a mine? Maybe if William managed a mine, he might let me work for him. I felt constrained by having to work inside. I longed to be back in the valley, helping with the hay making. Hay making brought everyone together and, though it was prickly and sweaty work, it was fun.

Since I couldn't be a part of it this year, I contrived time to go adventuring with the boys—to be out in the summer sunshine climbing the hills with them. It was as I was washing the children's faces in the cold water of the *Afon Caseg* that it occurred to me we could try and follow the river to its source. Just after midsummer, I rose with the sun and did all my chores before the boys woke. When they got up, I tied Tomos onto my back in an old shawl and gave Abner a basket, with a small picnic, to carry. We hadn't walked far before he was trying to get Arwel to carry it for him. We followed the river all the way up from Bethesda.

The higher we climbed the hotter the day got. It wasn't easy with a little one on my back. The boys bounded on ahead, swinging the basket in turns, and I half expected our picnic to be crumbs by the time we reached the source of the river. Bits of scree increased on the path until it was all scree and we had to be careful not to knock rocks into the river gully below us. We were near the source.

Around a huge boulder of rock we came and it was as if a door opened into a hidden world. There before us was a magnificent valley with a lake in the middle. The boys let out a whoop and ran towards the shore. The edge of the lake was clear and the rocks looked rusty beneath the water. The middle was inky black and deep.

We took our boots and stockings off and paddled. The cold was biting, but so welcome and refreshing after that unsteady clamber up the valley. I splashed some water on my face. We sat and ate the battered picnic on big boulders by the edge of the lake. When we had finished, Tomos sat in my lap. I counted his toes, tickled his feet and dipped them into the clear water. He splashed and giggled. The water spattered my skirts. He did it again.

Arwel and Abner were standing in the water by the rocks, doubled over with their heads together and hands in the water. They were trying to catch tiny minnows that darted through the shadows in the shallows. The mountains swept up to the skies all around us. It was heaven. We were hidden by the beauty of Carnedd Llewellyn that towered behind us and completely cut us off from the rest of the world. I thought what William might think of it.

I later learned that the lake was known as Mare's Fountain or *Ffynnon Caseg* as this was the valley where the mares came to foal—a secret. It felt so safe. Not a care in the world could touch me there. Arwel, Abner, Tomos and

I made it our favourite haunt all summer and, whenever we could, we would take a picnic and escape to refresh our feet in the Mare's Fountain.

At harvest time, Uncle John came to Bethesda. Dewi, Mrs Gruffudd, Tanwen and Owen came too. We showed them how Tomos had learnt to walk and how healthy Mared had become. It was lovely to see them all crowd out the cottage while the sun shone in through the windows I had buffed. They had come up the road, bringing cheerful news from Nant. Uncle John complimented me on my housekeeping and the happiness of the boys. He told me that William was well. Dewi was more content for having been in work and his boys were pleased to see him.

They weren't meant to stay long, but providence had it that before they left, baby Bryn was born. Owen ran for the midwife. The rest of us went outside and waited in the late summer sunshine. It all happened rather fast and I was relieved they were there. I stayed on to help Mared with baby Bryn, and Dewi came to and fro for weeks on end between Nant and Bethesda. Mam and Mrs Gruffudd still came regularly with supplies to help fill all the mouths. We settled into a comfortable routine. Mared sometimes took Dewi to chapel when he was home, but I always stayed back with the boys. It was a full year later before I said goodbye and promised to come and see them again. They hugged me, baby Bryn gurgled and Tomos clung to my skirts.

"No Eh-yin," he said.

Uncle John came to collect me. Arwel and Abner ran after the cart as we left, waving vigorously. I was sad to leave them but looked forward to returning to Nant.

What would be different? I had not seen Dad, or Ifan, or William or Ceinwen. I was looking forward to seeing William the most. Life in Bethesda had been so different and busy.

Book Two

Chapter One

Uncle John and Owen took me back as far as the farm. From there, I walked home but not before Owen showed me the little cottage they had built in the bottom pasture. It wasn't quite finished but it was good enough for him and Tanwen to move in. Their wedding was to be a few weeks after the harvest supper.

With his infectious grin breaking out, Owen took his cap off and waved goodbye from his new door. I turned towards the village. The sea, flat and open-armed before me, welcomed me back. Blackberries decorated the hedges and a smell of camomile and honeysuckle hinted that summer was nearly over. A figure with a crook in hand and a wooden box on his hip was walking slowly towards me, concentrating on each step by thoughtful step. He looked up.

"William!" I called and ran towards him. He had grown so tall.

"Elin, you're back."

I laughed.

"Your voice?" I was incredulous. "You sound like a man."

We both laughed and looked at each other as if we had met for the first time.

"I've missed you," he said.

"I have missed being in Nant," I replied, not having the courage to tell him how much I had missed him.

William turned and walked slowly with me towards the village.

"What was it like living in Bethesda?" he asked.

"Hard work!" I laughed.

I told him of Mared and baby Bryn, of Arwel, Abner and Tomos. I told him of the routine and the mundane pattern that life fell into. I had learnt a lot about babies and children. William was amused. I also told him how we found and frequently visited *Ffynnon Caseg*, hidden in its secret valley, how beautiful it was and how only the mares seemed to know about it.

"It sounds lovely," he said.

"I'll take you there, one day." We rested in a gateway and looked out to sea. "How are you William? What have you done while I have been gone?" I had to look up to him now he was so much taller and he had filled out like a man.

"Well now," he smiled, "I've not been idle, working for your Uncle John. We have had a good year. The lambs fetched a good price and this summer was kind." This was sensible grown-up talk!

"Has anything come of your gold mine?"

"Yes!" His excitement made me laugh and I saw that he had not changed. "I showed Owen the valley when we were looking for stones to build his cottage. It was an answer to prayer. He said he knew of someone he had met at an eisteddfod who might be able to help, a geologist. It took us until spring, this year, before we could to get down to Barmouth to see him; Mr Ellis his name is. We got to see one of the gold mines there that he has built. He was excited by our possible find but has yet to come and look at the prospect."

"That's wonderful news, William."

"I also have news that doesn't please me, Elin." He put a strong manly hand on my shoulder. Oh no! My heart dropped like a rock into the sea. What was it?

"Mr Price…" He paused to think over his words and my mind supplied the possibilities. Mr Price had got there first. Mr Price had the Take Note to open a mine in the valley and would steal all William's dreams from him. No?

"He has asked Non to marry him,"

"Non?"

William continued, "And she said yes."

"No!" I was horrified. My heart sank to the bottom of the seabed.

"He can't do that. He can't marry his *morwyn*. She is half his age." I was reminded of how Dad had been so antagonistic about the rumour of an understanding developing between Ceinwen and Rhodri because of their different positions. Ceinwen was an under laundry maid and Rhodri Parry an engineer. Now here was Non agreeing to marry the minister in whose household she had been a servant.

"It's unacceptable!"

One look at William assured me that he felt as uncomfortable about the idea as I did. So there were to be two weddings—two very different weddings. One would be full of comfort and encouragement. Owen and Tanwen's union would be celebrated with the approval of the village and families, but Non and Mr Price… I felt for William and his family.

The hedge behind us whispered slightly in the wind and rustled like the movement of country mice.

"What is she thinking?" I asked.

"I don't know."

She was such a sensible girl, warm and considerate. Her big heart was the first thing you got to know when you met her. Mr Price was cold and distant. He did not express affection for anyone very well.

William was watching me.

"You have caught the sun, Elin. Your scar has faded."

He was very matter-of-fact.

"Has it?" I fingered the scar on my eyebrow. It was old now and didn't make me feel as self-conscious as it used to. Hearing him say it had faded sounded more believable than when Llinos told me the same over a year ago. Maybe one day it would disappear altogether.

"I spent as much time outside with the boys as I could," I said.

"I'd love to see this *Ffynnon Caseg*, one day," he said. "One day," he said again, "we'll go; but for now, I'm sorry to say that I need to get on with work. Your Uncle will be wondering where I am, and you need to get on home. Your Mam will be pleased. It's wonderful to see you back." He squeezed my shoulder. "Come up to the farm when you can."

We parted and I came down into the village. The men were coming back from the quarry, and when I reached our door, I heard a familiar cough behind me.

"Dad!" I turned back on the threshold. He and Ifan were coming past the green towards the cottage.

"*Helo, Elin*!" Ifan called cheerfully across to me with a

wave.

I waited.

"You're back," Dad said gruffly as he came up by my shoulder and pushed the door open. Mam was inside bending over the range. She turned and saw me.

"Oh Elin!" There was comfort in her voice. I was home. *"Tyrd cariad."*

She drew me in, kissed me and hugged me tight, then sat me down on the settle, plying me with questions about Mared and the boys. Dad sat down heavily in the chair by the range while Ifan filled the coal scuttle for Mam and went to wash out at the back. Everything felt so familiar. Mam brought some potato and pies to the table. There was plenty to go around. Dad and Ifan must be doing well or perhaps they had a kinder manager.

"Dewi was a big help to your Dad," Mam explained. "He more than doubled the amount of rock your Dad and Ifan could quarry and helped Dad to negotiate some fair prices. They've been bringing home good wages."

Ifan and I helped Mam to clear and clean after our meal, while Dad sat. At each cough he moved a little closer to the coals and scrunched up tighter as he bent forward in the chair. I caught Ifan's eye and frowned. When we had finished rattling the crockery away, the cottage fell into a drowsy quiet. Mam put her mending on her knee and watched the fire.

"Elin!" Dad broke the silence and spouted a number of rasping coughs before carrying on.

"You can't stay here. You need to find a position of service."

He didn't want me. Mam and Ifan were looking at me.

I stared back at them, each in turn. I wanted to go back to how things had been before I had gone to Bethesda. I tugged at my collar. It felt uncomfortably tight. I wanted to be like Miss Evans and teach, to go back to school, anything but go into service.

"Where shall I look?" I asked submissively.

"Mrs Parry—in the morning." He coughed into the coals.

I wasn't going to argue with Dad. So the next morning, a maid who had been sweating over the laundry at the engineer's house directed me from the washroom to the kitchen to find Mrs Parry. The engineer's house was the biggest house in the village, bigger even than the minister's Manse. She received me stiffly and, when she heard why I had come, mentioned Non.

"I have no work here," she said, "but Mr Price, Gweinidog will need a new maid when he gets married." Her lips were pursed and her cheeks sucked sourly in. She looked me up and down very thoroughly. "I will speak to him." Her son, Rhodri, did not get his cheerful countenance from her.

To work at the Manse for Mr Price seemed more appealing. Non had always lived at home when she worked for him. If I could live at home, I could stay where everything was familiar. I was glad I didn't have to work for the engineer's wife, all in black with her high collar. When Dad returned I told him what Mrs Parry had said.

"No!" He was adamant. "You're not going to work there."

Was that because Mr Price was going to marry his servant? I looked to Mam and Ifan for help. Ifan stood up but didn't say anything.

"Keep looking, *cariad*," said Mam sympathetically. But before I set out to make enquiries at Plas Horon the next day, Mr Price came and spoke with Mam. She sent me out and whatever he said made Mam put on her armour and convince Dad to change his mind. It was settled that I would be a maid to the minister, Mr Price, Gweinidog, and his new wife, Non, when they got married.

The Price's wedding came and only a token of the village attended. It was a week after Owen and Tanwen's joyful gathering, which had been like a second harvest supper. Then he took her away to England. The leaves were changing colour and blowing from the trees to make a slushy mush on the track out of the village. I began my work in the Price's household before they came back. Cook was a small lady with a moon-shaped face and cherry-cake cheeks. She was kind. The gardener was like an old apple tree, gnarled, wrinkled and solid but very grumpy. He came into the kitchen at eleven for a cup of tea, every day, and had a good whinge and whine with Cook. That was the only time he came into the house.

When the Prices returned, the skies became permanently grey again and the days grew shorter. I got used to rising in the dark, before anyone at home had stirred, and making my way through the morning mists to the Manse. I would warm myself lighting and laying the fires, and by the time Mr Price and Non rose, the chill would have lifted.

One morning, as I was standing in the red study with

beeswax in my hand, Non wandered in. Gone was the mob cap. Her hair was turned up and rolled around her head. Her fancy lace collar and ladylike vestment did not either fit or suit her. It was as if she was playing a game of dressing up, trying to be like Mrs Parry.

"Elin." She nodded to me. There was an awkward silence between us. Non ran her finger across the top of the desk, turned the tip of it to the light and went and stood silhouetted in the window. Outside, the bland paste of sameness blended with her hollow figure. It was a dull day. She said nothing more and I watched her leave the room.

Later, I was laying the table in the dining room and she came in and rearranged the glasses. With a knife in her hand she looked at me. She didn't say a word but went around the table and swapped the position of every knife I had put down. It was like she was looking for work and companionship. I felt uncomfortable and uncertain of my place now I was her servant. She looked at me listlessly. Sometimes she would come and work beside me quietly, for want of better things to do.

She was nothing like the Non I had known before she got married. Her big, warm heart was hidden in a shadow of sadness and the change in her was hard to believe. I tried, but I found her difficult to engage in conversation. She didn't have anything she wanted to talk about. On the days when she would go out with Mr Price, she came back more deflated than before she left. When he was home, she seemed out of place and flitted aimlessly from room to room, rearranging this here and putting that there, quite unnecessarily.

It was one wet and windy Wednesday afternoon that William called with two baskets full of apples from the farm. There were cooking apples and small eating apples with skins of various hues. I answered the door.

"William," I cheered, making no effort to hide my delight at seeing him standing on the kitchen step.

"Come in, come in!" My arm was working like windmill sails turning the grindstone.

"I didn't think you would have had time to come up to the farm," he said, "and we were bringing some apples to the boat. I thought Non would like some, too."

He had come in the back door like a tradesman, so I left him to sample Cook's treats and went to find Non. Telling her William had come was like pouring cold water on a sleeping soul. She came to life and was so excited that she forgot herself and welcomed me into the parlour with William. I sat with them, not a servant, much to Cook's disgust, but as a friend. Non and William chatted away catching up with news over a tray of tea and cakes. I listened. There was no awkwardness in Non around William. The cheerful, warm-hearted girl I had once known was back. But as soon as William left, Non was gone too. In her place was an empty shell.

From then on, every Wednesday, William would drop by when he and Uncle John came down to the quay to meet the boat. Both Non and William liked me to be there—"Most irregular," according to Cook. I listened to them talk in familiar comfort as brother and sister. Non was herself again and I watched William talk to her as if she were a struggling ewe. He was always encouraging. It was a treat for me to see him and I waited impatiently for

Wednesdays.

Chapter Two

With rising early and returning late every day, it was almost as if I had actually left home. I barely saw Mam except to give her my wages, and I only ever saw the back of Dad's head as he crouched by the range. One night, I came in and there was a figure sitting in the chair. I thought Dad must have fallen asleep there. The coals were glowing. No light shone. But it was Ifan who turned around as I took my coat off.

"Elin?" He must have fallen asleep. He sounded disorientated.

"Ifan? Are you all right?"

There were shadows on his face. I crept closer to the coal light. He didn't look himself at all.

"I couldn't sleep," he said as I sat down on the settle and looked at him. I yawned. I'd be asleep in a few minutes.

Today, at Non's instruction, I had mixed linseed oil with treacle and alcohol and polished every piece of wooden furniture until my face shone back at me. My shoulder ached with the effort. The Manse was a big rambling old house, with lots of dark, hidden corners for me to clean. Tonight, as I waited at the table, I had listened to the conversation, if you can call it a conversation. It was one sided. Mr Price talked at Non, barely listening to her words. He had been down to Barmouth in the day to meet a gentleman there.

"It was only a small affair," he was saying. "About an acre, and the outbuildings were simple. They looked as if they had been built in a hurry. It would be easy to replicate. However, in order for the machinery to work there must be water," he repeated himself, "There must be water. That is paramount. We need to harness the water." And he thoughtfully chewed on the carpetbag steak Cook had made. Someone had come to the door selling mussels which Cook bought. It wasn't Llinos, but I did wonder if they were mussels that she had sold to Betsi. This was the time of year that she might look for mussels.

Non said nothing. She was watching her husband push his green beans around his plate.

"Water is powerful." He was talking with green beans in his mouth and gravy on his moustache. "I've been thinking ever since I went to Plas Tan y Bwlch—you know that they have electricity in the house there? Well, it is all generated by the river. Most ingenious!"

"How does that work?" Non asked.

Mr Price ignored her.

"I have been thinking—" he paused to chew, "if we were to harness the river here could we use it to produce electricity for the village?"

Non looked at him startled.

"Electricity," she said. "In the village? Whatever for?"

"Light! Of course!" He actually answered her question but the way he spoke implied he left off saying 'you fool'.

I missed the rest of the conversation. Cook had gone home and I had to finish washing the pots in the scullery. When I was done, I turned down the lamps and walked home. Frost was already starting to form and the cloudless night sky pushed the stars close.

The fire had been banked up with coals to last through the night, but I could see that Ifan was shivering. I reached out and vigorously rubbed the top of his arms.

"What is it?"

His voice was brittle. "There was an accident at the quarry today."

He stared into the coals. I said nothing. One of the coals dropped in the grate and a flame leapt up, illuminating Ifan's face. He looked broken.

"Who was hurt?" I eventually asked.

"Gareth Thomas."

There was silence. Only the coals spat and cackled a little with a fresh flame.

"We think he got his tamper mixed up with his jumper and there was a big explosion. Oh! It shouldn't have happened. I can't get his face out of my mind." Ifan began to cry. "Every time I close my eyes I see his face when the rock crushed him."

I took his hand. He grabbed mine hard.

"Stay with me, Elin. I can't sleep."

I went upstairs and pulled blankets from our beds. Wrapping one around Ifan in the chair, I lay down on the settle. It was cold and hard. I was so tired, I thought it would have been impossible not to sleep, but Ifan wanted to talk. He needed me to listen.

"Why? God, why? Why Gareth Thomas, of all people? His face, Elin, his face," he sobbed. "And now … gone, gone forever. I won't see him again. Where has he gone?" He rambled on repeating himself, moidering in his mind.

Ifan and Gareth had been friends forever, getting into mischief together—making bargains that if one had to wear the "Welsh Not" at school then the other had to speak Welsh and wear it too—until eventually they had grown out of their mischief and were working side by side with their fathers in the quarry, making bargains on rock. They were the closest of friends.

"He's gone to heaven, Ifan," I answered hoping to settle his qualms.

"Has he?"

I kept drifting into uneasy sleep, not too sure if I was awake or asleep. The night got colder and colder, and when it was coldest, I knew it was time to get up. I was still fully dressed, so I rose and poked the fire. My eyes felt grainy under my lids, like they needed dusting, and my head was heavy. Ifan was still awake. He didn't move. He watched me. A cough and a step on the stairs announced that Dad was up earlier than usual.

"*Wfft*, have you two been up all night?" Dad asked when he saw the blankets. Putting on my coat, I excused myself and went out.

The moon was low and shone an eerie light on the frost. It sparkled high in the trees. Bitterly cold air refreshed my head and blew at my crusty eyes. I stepped cautiously around the puddles of iron, but when I reached the flagstones to the back door of the Manse, I slipped. Grabbing a drain pipe, I grazed my knuckles on the wall and felt so foolish. When I got into the kitchen, I sat down and cried. I was tired but that wasn't all: I cried for Ifan. He had lost a special friend. The blood was running from my graze and I smeared it across my face as I rubbed

111

my eyes. My reflection stared back at me from a copper kettle in horror. I went back outside, broke the ice on the water trough, washed the blood and tears from my face, ran my fingers through my hair and tried to make myself presentable. With some muslin wrapped around my wound, I lit the fires in all the rooms slowly thawing the cold that gripped me.

It stayed icy all day and the gardener moaned about the hard ground when he came in for his morning tea. A young gardener from Plas Horon was being sent to collect some seeds, he told us. Would we tell him when he arrived? He muttered that he wished Plas Horon were sending him a young gardener to help. Although I heard him say this, it was still a surprise to find Ceinwen's redheaded friend, Huw, talking to Cook when I came into the kitchen later that morning.

"Hello, Elin." He remembered my name.

"*Helo*."

"Have you heard about the accident at the quarry?"

I nodded. "My brother's friend, Gareth, died," I said.

"Oh. I am so sorry." I looked at him sharply and his face was genuinely sympathetic. "I'll be praying for your family," he said, simply. I felt a rush of warmth for this young gardener.

Mr Price, Gweinidog conducted the funeral, and the entire village turned out to meet the Thomas family's grief with condolences. It was then that I noticed that no one in the village spoke to Non. I was beside Ifan at the grave, when I looked across and saw her standing with her head down alone next to the cemetery wall. She sat alone in chapel, too, her hat hiding her eyes, and no one spoke to her there either.

I was glad when William called the following Wednesday.

"Non, is not happy." I told him, although he already knew.

Later I found her sitting in the weak sunlight with her neck cricked, looking at her hands. She hiccupped and wiped her nose. I put my bucket down in the hallway and stepped into the room. There were streaks on her cheeks. At the sight of me, Non shook her head and began to cry harder. I put my arms around her and she cried on my shoulder. I held her until it felt like the storm was passing; then she began to pull herself together.

"I'm sorry," she eventually said.

I shook my head. There was nothing to be sorry for. Grief was a familiar part of our life. It felt very present at that moment, but something told me Non wasn't crying in grief for Gareth Thomas. Ifan was still struggling to muster his strength every morning and return to work at the quarry that was empty of Gareth's companionship. They had been so close. Dad had been affected too. He was drinking more, Ifan said. But it was something else that had upset Non, I could see.

"What is it?" I asked.

"What have I done, Elin? Why did I marry him?" Non was on the brink of more tears.

I had no answer.

"I thought it would be good, but he is so distant and still treats me as a servant not his wife," she sobbed. "I try hard to do everything right. But nothing is right. No one treats me like they used to." After a long pause, she said, "Except William. Mam won't come because the house is too grand and no one talks to me the same. They think I am fancy, but I haven't changed, Elin. Now no one talks to me at all." She pitied herself.

It was difficult. She had crossed boundaries and entered territories she was unprepared for. I had found it difficult to know where the borders were between servant and friend; difficult to know when or how I should talk to her. She had struggled too. I still found it difficult, but couldn't say so; instead, I offered a comforting arm. I knew no better than her what the answer was.

From that day on, she seemed to decline inside her shell even more. She went out less, got up later and looked pasty and ill. She kept being sick until Doctor Salusbury came.

Doctor Salusbury was the doctor everyone in Nant saw, even Mr Parry. He was employed by the quarry to attend all the quarrymen and their families. There was a scheme to cover his fees that had come about when the new terraces were built, along with a system of using tokens in Mr Hughes' grocery shop. The Ithfaen Quarry looked after their employees better than Lord Penrhyn.

Doctor Salusbury said he had good news. A little Price was growing inside Non and all would be well. However, the days that followed did not feel "well." Mr Price crashed around the house while it rained heavily and turned everything to mud. He invited his friend from Barmouth to come and visit, but the friend never came, and that put him in a sour temper. He took no interest in how Non was feeling. When I listened to him speak with great loftiness over the top of our heads in chapel, exhorting us to do good and remain faithful to virtues in the Bible, I wondered at his blundering selfishness. At home, he seemed unaware of anyone but himself.

Watching the water rill in runnels from the sheets I wrangled with and hung to dry on a clear day, I thought about his talk of electricity. Why would the village need electricity? What good would it bring? It would not make life in the quarry any easier, surely. Electricity could not have saved Gareth Thomas.

When I turned the sheets through the mangle, the light caught the remaining drips that squeezed out, and the sun turned them to gold. I looked up at the bracken-covered mountain behind the village. The mangle slowed. I would give anything to be running with the wind through that rustling bracken. The beautiful mountains passed through my mind in pictures. I thought of William, with the freedom he still had to explore the hills. It would be getting close to lambing time again, and then the buds would break in the hedges and the leaves would come out. I listened to the blackbird trilling to the approaching dusk. Spring was on the way.

Non began to blossom under her bodice and she asked me to live-in, in a room in the attic. Officially, I left home, which had no longer felt like home since I had come back from Bethesda. No more did my little room in the Manse attic feel like home. I could not imagine living there forever. Maybe one day I could work in a mine.

William still came to see Non, but I stopped sitting in on his visits. There was too much to do. Then, one Wednesday, just before he departed, he caught me by the arm, in the kitchen. Cook was in the garden. He pulled me close and whispered in my ear,

"Mr Ellis, the geologist, came."

"And?"

"He said it's real gold, not fool's gold and he was very excited. He is going to bring another man to see it."

A footfall in the passage outside the door threw us apart. He grabbed his cap, rammed it on his head saying, "Come to Mynydd Seion on Sunday. I'll tell you more about it then." The door slammed. He was gone. At the same time the kitchen door opened and Mr Price walked in.

"Has William gone?" he asked.

"Yes, but only just," I replied, stepping towards the door to call William back. When had the minister returned home and how did he know William was here?

"It's all right," Mr Price said. "I'll catch him another time. Tell me when he comes again."

He turned and was gone.

Chapter Three

Dad was at the door of the Manse. It wasn't me he had come to see.

"Is Mr Price in?" he asked.

"No."

"Tell him," Dad stopped to cough, "I have done what he asked for."

No 'Hello Elin. How are you? It's nice to see you.' I sighed.

"Yes Dad. I'll tell him. How are you?"

"*Iawn*. I'm fine." He coughed again. Dad looked gaunt. You're not fine, I thought to myself.

I knew when Mr Price was home for I could hear him telling Non that he was all about innovation and bringing something refreshing to the village. It was all 'I' this and 'I' that—all about him. A cockerel strutting around came to mind. I went to pass on Dad's message but he saw my shadow by the study door and called to me before I got there.

"Elin, tell Cook that Mr Ellis, from Barmouth, is coming to stay, on Monday. He'll be with us until Wednesday."

"Yes, sir," I said and gave Dad's message.

"Good! Good! It's all coming together," he said rubbing his hands.

I went and found Cook straight away. She muttered something about having enough to do already. It wasn't like Cook to complain, but we had been busy getting the nursery ready for Non.

The household mood brightened. His friend's impending visit made Mr Price more cheerful and he showed Non some consideration by listening to her when she spoke. I was excited too and looking forward to visiting Mynydd Seion, in Trem y Mynydd, as William had invited me. I wanted to hear what he had to say about the gold but I was also curious about the chapel there. Something was happening. 'Revival' some people called it, 'hysteria' others said. Ceinwen had said she 'met' Jesus there. People did not talk like that in our chapel, and I had found something comforting in the hymn singing and praying when I went before, with Uncle John. Tired by Non's loneliness and Mr Price's tetchiness, I wanted an excuse to escape over the brow of the mountains and see my favourite views again.

When I told Non that I was going to the chapel in Trem y Mynydd she looked pained, like I had betrayed her. The rain tried to deter me, too, by spitting at me and little fingers of wind attempted to scratch their way beneath my coat. I was having none of that nonsense. I buttoned up tight. By the time I reached the other side of the woods, the weather flopped a pessimistic blanket of drizzle on me. Little beads of moisture stood out on the fibres of my woollen coat, like drops of perspiration.

In Trem y Mynydd, I met with others whose purpose bent them in the same direction as me, blown by the offshore breeze towards the thin arched windows at the end of the street. There was not a face amongst them that I recognised beneath hats and caps, their collars cupping their cheeks. They called cheerful greetings to one another.

It had been so long since I had seen Uncle John or Ceinwen but when I got into the dry, I still could not find a familiar face. I climbed up to the gallery and found a dusty corner to hide myself in. There was a holy anticipation, a sort of reverent silence, as if something great was about to happen, and as soon as the singing began, the back of my neck tingled and my heart vibrated.

They were singing the same hymn they'd sung the last time I had come. I joined in with the refrain, *If I've Jesus, Jesus only*, and listened to the words I didn't know.

> *"What though all my earthly journey*
> *Brings me naught but weary hours"*

My journey had certainly brought me some weary hours since I last came to this place.

> *"And, in grasping for life's roses,*
> *Thorns I find instead of flowers"*

Ifan and Non, I thought of them and the grief they had both grasped that had pricked and pained them, just like a thorn.

> *"If I've Jesus, "Jesus only,"*
> *I'll possess a cluster rare;*
> *He's the "Lily of the Valley,"*
> *And the "Rose of Sharon" fair"*

Ceinwen and William claimed they had met Jesus and that he was rare treasure, like a beautiful bunch of flowers.

I sighed and closed my eyes. I had come home to rest, just sitting there, listening in a corner someone forgot to dust—a dove contentedly at roost in a dovecote. Here was peace. Here was home.

The service flowed from one thing to the next, with seamless effort. Who was leading it? It wasn't the minister, although his hands were often raised in prayer. People in the congregation freely contributed prayers, hymns and texts from the Bible whenever they wanted, and all had a common thread to them. Rhodri Parry got up and spoke. He was his father's son and spoke with such authority that I was compelled to listen. He spoke directly to me, as if I was the only one in the room.

"Jesus said, "Follow me," he quoted, *"and I will make you fishers of men".* I will give your life purpose," he interpreted.

I peeped a little further over the gallery and there saw Ceinwen. She was sitting next to that redheaded gardener Huw *Piws*. She looked beautiful. Peace surrounded her too and it was as if she sat in golden light, only it did not come from the window but from within her and shone out of her.

There was something thick and heavy lingering in the atmosphere, a sense of permanence, and I did not want to move. When the heavy presence lifted, the service came to an end. Through the windows the sun shone. The rain had gone. I could see the mountainside was clean of clouds. I was drawn out of my dusty corner by the sight of smiling faces and I descended the stairs to find William grinning at me. He said he had just seen Ceinwen leave. I stepped outside quickly to find her. Ceinwen? She wasn't anywhere. I had missed her. Where was Uncle John? There were so many people.

William caught my elbow and nudged me to the side where the crowd thinned. When we were right on the edge he asked me,

"Have you got time to spare today?"

I nodded. Pleased, he led me towards the track that took us out of the back of the village and up the mountain. "Come and share my *cinio*. Let's climb to Tre'r Ceiri," he said.

Up we went—not a difficult climb. The heather grew tall on the hillside. I put my hand out to rattle the little bells and wanted to whoop with exuberance. I was out on the fresh threshold of spring, with no responsibility for a moment. Once again, I was following William.

The mountainside rose a little steeper before a ridge and wall that formed the outer boundary of the ancient fort of Tre'r Ceiri. Inside were the remains of stone huts. Their walls were not high, but they were everywhere. We clambered from one to the next until we reached the opposite side of the fort and looked down the steep black rock that dropped away to the farmland beyond. The view from that edge was the inspiration of legends, and beyond, laid out flat, was an expanse that caught the imagination of artists. We climbed up higher to the left, and from there could see every aspect of the peninsula, catching the light. The wind blew my breath away and I leant into it laughing, to see if it could take my weight and hold me. I stumbled and William caught me, his laughter disappearing down the mountainside. The wind was playing rough games, so we turned back down towards the ruined huts where some men had begun to work. Archaeologists, William called them, not geologists. He said they were digging up the past to see if they could find out who the people were and how they lived in those huts, all those ancient years ago. Some of the ruins were round and some were rectangular.

Sheltered from the wind, William sat in the ruins of a square-shaped dwelling, leaning his back against the stone wall. The sea around the peninsula was patched with dark shadows of clouds. Everything looked colourful and textured like a fancy oil painting, with blues and greys and greens, slight hues of purple, and the white in the sky. It was very beautiful.

I leant against the wall, leaving at least three feet between William and me. He teased my awkwardness and joked, saying he would not eat me if I sat by him.

"Tell me about this man who came to see the valley and told you it is real gold," I said.

"Mr Ellis?" He looked at me. "Sit down, Elin."

I sat a little closer to him on the loose stones by the wall and William handed me a piece of pie.

"Mr Ellis was the man Owen and I went to see, in Barmouth, in the summer. He knows a good deal. He is a geologist and manager of Gwynaber Mine. It is only small and he built it up himself, but he had help from a company in London and a prospector called Mr Morgan to finance it. He is thinking of expanding and is interested in what we showed him here, above Nant. He is staying in Caernarfon at the moment and says he's waiting for Mr Morgan, the prospector from Hugo Cranmer & Sons, to come up from London."

"That sounds promising," I said.

"The Company want to survey the area and then if there are prospects they will raise interest," he said. "I don't know how long it will take. Mr Ellis is bringing Mr Morgan, as soon as he arrives, to survey the valley with him."

He nonchalantly threw a small pebble, listening to it ring against the boundary stone of the outer wall.

"If the mine goes ahead, Mr Ellis has promised me an apprenticeship, Elin," he said.

"That's wonderful! Does Uncle John know?"

"I haven't said anything to him, but Owen might have. He is interested too. I think he sees the potential. He thinks a mine there will be good for the village; it will bring more work and money, which is positive progress. Owen thinks that this area needs something fresh, organised by ordinary not fancy folk—people like you and me Elin, not the Lloyds or Penrhyns. When you next have a day out, come to the farm and I'll take you up to the valley. I'll show you what Mr Ellis has shown me, and hopefully by then Mr Ellis will have brought Mr Morgan and we will know more."

I liked the sound of that—next month, then? I only got a day out once a month. It was agreed.

We fell silent. William, an apprentice gold miner was a step in the right direction. Our lunch sat contented in our bellies and a sleepy Sunday afternoon rest swept over us. William pulled his cap partly over his face and dozed. The broad span of a kite swooped and dropped down on prey. Moments later, it stood hunched over its kill, tearing at flesh between its feet. With a single flap it lifted back into the air and rose, carried off in the grace of the wind. Above it, several birds of prey circled on a warm thermal.

William stirred; the stones he sat on rattled against each other.

"Sorry Elin," he apologised.

"Sleep on!
*Huna blentyn, nid oes yma
Ddim i roddi iti fraw.*"

I sang and he chuckled.

"I haven't heard that for years."

"No. You don't need nursery rhymes and lullabies to send you to sleep now. All your hard work does that," I teased. "You'll be an Uncle soon." William as an Uncle wasn't too hard to imagine. He would be good, like my Uncle. The nursery was ready.

"Non isn't happy, William," I said. "You know that, don't you?"

"It's hard for us, too," he replied sadly, scratching the stone beside him. "Mam finds it very difficult. She doesn't like Mr Price, Gweinidog. She did not want Non to marry him."

I could understand.

"Then why did your parents let her?" I asked.

"Non had said it was her only chance of marriage. She told them that the prospects were too good to turn down. I don't know how she persuaded them, but she has made her own bed and now she must lie in it."

That was harsh. He heard my thoughts.

"I do care about her, Elin. Why else do I come every week to see her? But she has to bear the consequence of her choices. We all do."

He was right. I didn't like it. Non who had once seemed so wise in my eyes had made a bad decision and now she lived with it.

"What did you think of chapel, today?" William asked.

I mulled over my words carefully, trying to find the best ones, and those that came described how restful and refreshing chapel had felt: the anticipation, the excitement and the peace. It had been like drinking from the still waters of Ffynnon Caseg, filling and refreshing me from the inside out. It was like I had sat with my worn feet dipped in the cool water and seen the dust of dreary days wash off and float away. I had felt free from cares throughout the service only aware of being in the present. What was past had passed and what was to come was nothing to be afraid or worried by.

"That's the presence of God." William was excited by my description. "And," he looked at the sun, "it's nearly time for chapel. Will you come again?"

"I would love to, but I think I ought to go back to your sister. She wasn't too pleased with me for leaving her, today."

"You live-in now, don't you?"

I nodded.

"Mam and I are glad you're with her. Before you go, I want you to have this." He rustled with the remains of his lunch and brought out a well-worn Bible from amongst them. My stomach leapt inside me as he placed it in my lap. I picked it up and turned it in my hands. It was leather bound and looked expensive.

"I can't take it." I handed it back to him. "It's yours." He put out both his palms as a barrier.

"I want you to have it." He paused "… I feel very sure you are going to need it."

"We have a Bible at home." I was defensive. "If I need one, I can use that."

"No. I want you to have mine."

It did not make sense. Mr Price had shelves of books and amongst them, Bibles. I didn't have time to read. But there was something in his eyes that meant I couldn't refuse.

Chapter Four

With egg white and sugar, I cleaned all the leather in the spare bedroom, opened the windows wide to air the room before putting fresh linen on the bed. I laid the fire and found a chamber pot and warming pan ready for Mr Ellis. He had a rough ride and was blown in with a storm after dark. Mr Price hardly let him catch his breath before I could hear them talking over whisky and a warm fire. Non sat in the corner. She was more rounded now and her days were sedentary.

In the hallway, I brushed the rain and mud from Mr Ellis' coat that hung beneath his trilby on the hat stand.

"Have you sufficient capital to build a mill beside the river?" Mr Ellis asked. "And how well does that river run? Is it consistent throughout the year?"

"Now, therein lies a problem," came a muffled reply. "But, on my recent visit to Plas Tan y Bwlch, Oakley took me to see his dam on the lake. It is a feat of engineering and it gave me an idea. You know he had it built for his daughter's twenty-first birthday present years ago, don't you? He's quite mad, that fellow."

I left the hallway. There was no doubt Mr Ellis and Mr Price were discussing building a mine. Mr Ellis! Was this the same Mr Ellis William had met with? In which case, what was he doing here talking to Mr Price? William had said his Mr Ellis was going to consult a man from London. I shivered.

A cold blast of air hit me as I walked into the kitchen. Cook stood looking bewildered. The door was wide open and there was Ifan, dripping wet.

"Ifan?" I exclaimed in surprise.

He came into the kitchen and slammed the door behind him.

"Your Dad's taken bad, Elin," Cook was saying. "Ifan came to tell you."

"Not now," I panicked, feeling disorientated. "We have a guest here."

"He's sick—very sick." Ifan looked at me out of troubled eyes, so like Dad's. "You need to come, Elin. It's silicosis." He whispered. I froze. Dad's dry cough had become such a familiar sound that we didn't notice it anymore. "He's slipping fast."

"What...?" I couldn't bring myself to say it. He's dying?

"Yes, Elin come."

Cook interrupted.

"You can go when food is finished. I'll stay late and do the pots for you."

Ifan left and I went through the motions of serving a meal to Non, Mr Ellis and Mr Price. I did not concentrate. I was at home in a darkened room, fearing for Mam and Dad.

Non sat quietly and ate little, while Mr Ellis and Mr Price ate much and talked of railway lines, gauges and breaking terrain; of Cambrian and Caradocian sills; of calcite, pyrite, magnetite, hematite and potash feldspar. I'm sure Non understood as little as I did. As soon as they had withdrawn from the dining room and I had removed the last dish, I grabbed my coat and hat and ran. The rain stung and pricked my face. It flew at me horizontally. Upsurges of breakers were crashing on the beach and the noise carried on the wind.

I stumbled up the stairs at home and blundered into the room. A single candle gave off feeble light beside the bed. I could not believe it. They were all there. I was the last to come. Dad's eyes were shut and his breathing rattled. Mam held his hand. This was the man who had worked hard, kept his distance, drunk for comfort and been fierce in his pride but who now lay dying from the quarry dust he had worked with.

We sat altogether. Ceinwen's eyes glistened with emotion. The candle burned down and we waited, listening to Dad's rattle. I felt all mixed up and restless. I went downstairs and looked around the room for a job, any job that needed doing. Ceinwen followed me.

"You can't hide, Elin," she said. "The end will come."

"I don't want to see." I began to cry.

"What are you afraid of?" Ceinwen spoke gently.

"I don't know." My crying was cracked and dry but I couldn't hold it back.

She sat me down.

"There's nothing to fear," she said quietly in my ear.

But that was all I felt, fear, and I could not say why. What was I afraid of? Was it death that terrified me or was it the idea of another loss? For Dad, I felt nothing, but something scared me. I was mixed up with confusion and to add to it, was that Mr Ellis staying with Mr Price the same one William knew? I felt sick.

"I don't know what to think," I sobbed.

"Then don't!" Ceinwen advised.

It was a long night. The storm blustered and howled, and in the early hours of the morning Dad rattled his last rasping breath. I returned to the Manse.

Non said she was sorry and she meant it, but she was preoccupied. I only understood why when she asked me to go and find her Mam. I crossed the village with heavy limbs to the cottage where William and Non grew up. Mrs Williams was there, thankfully, in the back with a posher and dolly in a zinc tub. She met me with sympathy about Dad and the same look William would have given me, but when I explained I had come because Non was having pains, Mrs Williams was quick to put the water to cool and the clothes to hang. She gathered a clean apron and some muslin cloths, muttering to herself:

"*Dydy o ddim yr amser.*"

She came back with me and told me what to do. I was glad. I had no strength for initiative. The doctor came and Mr Price was pacing the hallway, unsure where to put himself. Mr Ellis left out of courtesy and as he went I heard him say he was waiting for news from Nathaniel Morgan who was coming up from London. He was the same Mr Ellis!

Non was at risk of delivering her baby early, the doctor had said, and he confined her to her bed for permanent rest. He assigned her mother the role of nurse and Mrs Williams stayed at the Manse.

Spring was now in a full fling of pastel colours, but on

the day we gathered to commit Dad back to the dust it was sombre and grey. Mam carried her widow's weeds with her no-nonsense approach and stalwart strength. Ifan supported her, holding her by the arm and guiding her round with dignity. Dewi came with Mared and their boys. My smiles to Arwel, Abner and Tomos were weak but they warmly greeted me. People spoke great things of Dad. Their words were feathers in my ears for they did not speak of the Dad I had known. Dad never liked me. He drank himself senseless and did not care much. No one said they were ashamed of him, but I was. I thought Ceinwen would understand.

"What they are saying doesn't make sense." I whispered, the felt of my hat touching hers. "Aren't you ashamed of Dad? He was rough with you, Ceinwen."

She surprised me.

"No, I forgave him long ago. He was a sad man," she said and looped her arm through Llinos' as we stood to sing a hymn. I looked at Llinos' face. It was like a blanket of whitewash. I could not tell what she was thinking. Some people stared at her.

William came and stood beside me in the cemetery, handing me a pink and white dog rose that had flowered early in the walled orchard of the farm. The petals were shaped like hearts. I didn't want to put it on the coffin so I threaded it into the button hole on my coat and he smiled.

There was just enough space beyond the little mounds of baby graves for Dad to be buried by Bethan's headstone. I waited behind as everyone walked back into the village for tea and cakes in the schoolroom. William waited with me. I was going to tell him about Mr Ellis but when I met the compassion in his eyes, I burst into tears. He drew me against his chest and held me. His arms were strong and safe. My eyes swelled and my nose ran. I felt even more confused. He handed me his handkerchief and we walked back into the village in silence. The dog rose in my button hole was crushed.

I had always felt that Dad had weighed us down as a family, but oddly now that he was gone, I felt heavier. I worried about Mam though Ifan assured me he was looking after her. The days were close and sweaty. It was a warm spring and I had little enthusiasm for my daily chores. I longed for something to change.

"Your father was a good man," Mr Price had said to me when we returned to the Manse after the funeral. I kept my thoughts to myself.

"I knew him when I was a boy. He used to come to my father's chapel and sometimes ate in our home with us. My father thought very highly of him and would let him preach. His fiancé died of pneumonia and he left the valley to move back up north, but I am sure he must have told you the story before. I was amazed to find him again. He was helping me with a project where his knowledge of explosives was second to none," he had said before returning to his study.

Dad was a surprising man but I still couldn't call him good. He was going to marry someone else before he met Mam, and he had preached in chapel. That was definitely not the Dad I knew. His heart must have broken when his fiancé died, and maybe he turned away from God, for I had never known him to go to chapel, let alone preach. In fact, he never spoke of God. Contrary to what Mr Price thought, I had not heard that story before.

"Elin, will you give this to your mother?" Mr Price came out of his study with a small package in his hand. "I owed it to your father."

There were coins in it.

Chapter Five

The following Wednesday, Mrs Williams opened the front door to William.

"*Fy mab*!" She kissed him.

I hung back in the shadows, wanting to speak to him, but he and Mrs Williams were talking and he went straight up to Non's room before I dared to emerge. Non was still in the safe haven of bed rest and every day drew her closer to delivery. I was cleaning the windows in the hallway with vinegar and newspaper when I heard Mr Price call to me from his study.

"Elin, where is my fountain pen?"

I went to the door.

"I'm sorry." I said, "I haven't seen it, sir."

Mr Price rapidly opened and shut all the draws in his desk. Banging loudly, he put his frustration into each one.

"You must have done. I left it here on my desk."

I turned around to go and there was William, cap in hand smiling at me.

"You wanted to see me, sir." He said.

"Ah, William." Mr Price had seen him too. "Come in."

Disconcerted, I brushed past him out of the study and back to the windows, where I tried to eliminate all smears of dirt or vinegar. I rubbed with deliberate downward strokes until I needed a fresh piece of newspaper. October 16th 1903, a column in the paper caught my eye. It was all about a new chapel being built in Bangor. Mr Lloyd George had given a speech. I read down to see what he'd had to say. It was a patriotic speech about the importance of Nonconformism in Wales. He said that Nonconformism was to the Welsh what the French Revolution was to the French. He named a number of preachers who were heroes in Welsh minds and said the most important thing in a chapel was that it provided somewhere to preach. He did not believe that Nonconformity was on the down grade, as some people said. What sort of a message did Dad preach when he preached down south?

I could hear the rumble of voices, down the passage. Their conversation went on and on. I was cleaning the porch by the time William came back. I had been recalling the sense of security and his strength and comfort I had felt when he held me close after Dad's funeral. He did not realise I was there and, as he came out, he tripped over my boot. His face was ashen. He was shaking.

"William! What is it?"

"He's told me to stay out of it," he retorted. "He says I'm a threat to his business and his plans."

"To the mine?"

"Yes, to the mine."

"But I thought…" At that moment, I heard Mrs Williams calling with great urgency.

"Elin! Elin!" I ran up the stairs. She was on the landing.

"Run for the Doctor will you, please." Anxiety screamed out to me from behind her façade of calm efficiency. "Be as quick as you can," she called to my retreating figure, and

I ran down the stairs. William was still outside.

"The Doctor for Non—" I said breathlessly, glimpsing the tautness in his face.

"I'll come." He put his cap on and the colour returned to his cheeks.

William found Dr. Salusbury before I did. He was at the Manse with Non when I got back and William had gone. Mr Price was pacing. Again, he did not know where to place himself. Mrs Williams told me to boil up some pans of hot water and help Cook prepare food as usual, so I made myself busy in the kitchen. Cook prattled on about the various children she had seen delivered. I shut out her chatter and thought of William, angry. Had Mr Ellis told Mr Price about William? Mr Ellis had promised William an apprenticeship. I was confused. Who was in charge and what was going on?

Food was ready but there was no call for it. I sought Mr Price and asked him if he wanted to eat, but he was so uptight he barely heard me and dismissed my offer with a waft of his hand. I went back to my normal chores. The house was holding its breath. Later, Mrs Williams came for the water and told me that the Doctor was still with Non. She looked like a grey rag herself, in contrast to the white sheet she was tearing into strips. I helped her; with a little tear at the top, the weft would wrench apart and the warp would make a nice straight strip.

After she left, I sat down. There was nothing left to do. Cook was dozing by the fire. The chair creaked. Occasionally, I could hear Non's pain. It twisted my heart.

BANG! Something hit the bottom of the sash window. I rose up and started forward to see what it was. The gardener was in the potting shed. No one else was there. I looked out. The patched blue sky beamed with sunshine. The sea was glossy. Everything looked calm and content. I picked up William's Bible from where I had left it on the windowsill and held it gently in my hands. With the spine cupped, I fanned through the pages until it fell open roughly in the middle. My hands sensed the need to treasure it and I held it tenderly. The blurred words on the page began to distinguish themselves.

> *My dove in the clefts of the rock,*
> *in the hiding places on the mountainside,*
> *show me your face,*
> *let me hear your voice;*
> *for your voice is sweet,*
> *and your face is lovely.*
>
> *(Song of Solomon 2:14)*

William had written beside, the words "*God's desire to hear our prayers*". There was much of William's small, precise handwriting pencilled between and beside the lines. I flipped a leaf back and understood I was reading part of a song. Beneath the black bold title, *Caniad Solomon*, William had written "God's love letter to us". God's love letter: was that like a love spoon, given to show the skill of a carver? Jonny had given Llinos a handmade love spoon after he had been away for a long time, out on his boat. It seemed to stir her before they got married. "*My dove,*" I read again, "*let me hear your voice; For your voice is sweet, And your face is lovely.*" It was the poetic language of a lover. I tried to memorise it.

As I put the Bible down on the windowsill, a gust of air blew the page, lifting it to flutter, a whisper, and I saw movement on the grass outside. Lying there was a stunned, scruffy-feathered blackbird fledgling breathing very rapidly. I rushed out of the back door and picked it up. Its little body was heaving up and down grasping breath, and the fluff of feathers trembled. I stroked it.

At that moment I heard a noise from an upstairs window that reminded me of the plaintive bleat of a newborn lamb. It wasn't strong, but it was a cry. The little bird opened its beak and looked at me. It shuffled its feathers and with a flick of the wings was gone from my hand into the safety of the hedge beyond the grass. Goodbye, little blackbird! Just in time; the ginger stripe of a cat came skulking around the corner.

Chapter Six

There was no laughter at his birth, but still they called him Isaac. Non looked drained and pale with the pain she had borne. I thought they would have done better to have named him Jabez, after his father. He was a long, scrawny little baby who screwed up his pink face and mewed in disgust at the world around him. It took a lot of coercion to convince him to settle to sleep and give Non rest. Mr Price, Gweinidog, strutted in pride at being a father, and a father of a boy, no less. He looked in on the mother and child and was off to share his good news with the world. The lines of anxiety etched darker on Mrs Williams' face, when all was done. She had aged. I congratulated her on becoming a *Nain*.

There followed days where life completely changed and the household revolved around young Isaac. His demands became the centre of the universe. With the three of us to attend to him, it was little wonder he thought he was Lord of the Manor, but Non was not recovering well and Mrs Williams looked more anxious.

Mr Price, on the other hand, kept his distance. "Not good!" I thought, remembering Dad. To hear him talk to the world outside, you would think Isaac was the most comely and bonny lad ever to be born. I looked into that little face, with eyes that barely opened, and struggled to agree. He was an ugly mite, long and scrawny, all fingers and toes, and when you dressed him his thin leg would lift up and down like he was stamping his oversized Rumpelstiltskin foot, while he cried. The way Mr Price acted reminded me of the saying, "*Gwyn y gwel y fran ei chyw er fod ei liw yn olau ddu*". The old crow most definitely saw beauty in his offspring that others didn't. Non was the same. Despite her pain, Isaac was the most wonderful thing that had ever happened to her—or so I heard her cooing to him, when he was quiet.

Feeding involved many tears, both from Non and Isaac, so Mrs Williams sent me to Mam Meredith's for salve and gripe water.

I set off on the stony road out of the village, climbing up out of the valley, on my way to Trem y Mynydd and, once again, I felt the relief of climbing high.

> *My dove in the clefts of the rock,*
> *in the hiding places on the mountainside,*
> *show me your face,*
> *let me hear your voice;*
> *for your voice is sweet,*
> *and your face is lovely.*
>
> *(Song of Solomon 2:14)*

The words were printed in my mind.

I looked across to Carreg Du, where the boulders cast shadows. These mountains held secrets from every generation. Isaac was the beginning of a new story and yet we hadn't finished unearthing the story of gold hidden in the mountainside where the *nant* ran.

I reached the edge of Trem y Mynydd. Mam Meredith provided the service of an old wife in keeping with tales told, and her simple herbal remedies were used by everyone. Mam had gone to her when I had fallen on the hay tedder and cut my eyebrow open. Her skills were different from those of the doctor, and she had answers for more commonplace ailments. She had given Mam a salve for my wound and later one for my scar. Who knew if the doctor would have helped my wound to heal better? I touched my familiar scar. It was a deep and lasting reminder of a small accident, a careless moment now with me for life.

Mam Meredith's garden was a profusion of sweet-scented flowers and herbs, and her long, low white cottage nestled behind the foliage like a rabbit trying to remain inconspicuous. I passed through the village, glancing at the chapel as I went. It was such a simple building to gather in, without all the grand, ornate stonework of St Beuno's down by the cliff tops at Pen-y-bont. St Beuno's had been there forever, and only fancy people went there now.

When I reached the hemline of the village, I turned down a little track beside a spinney, just before the Caernarfon road, and there was Mam Meredith, in her garden. She welcomed me into her cool cottage.

"What can I do for you today?" she asked.

As I explained Non's discomfort and how Isaac's colicky crying was turning Mrs Williams' hair white, Mam Meredith laughed with me. She said that a little dill water should help the gripes and some comfrey salve would soothe Non.

Her cottage was small and simple. It was neat and

homely, but distinctly lonely. Her husband was said to be with the regiment in Africa. He'd not returned after victory was declared and had been out there since before the old Queen had died. I'd never seen him. Dad once said the army was for those who couldn't quarry.

There were a few flowers in a glass bottle on the windowsill, a dark wood table in the centre of the room and a single chair. A round rag rug lay by the hearth and the wooden beams were decorated with hooks and drying herbs. It smelt lovely. Mam Meredith had gone into the room adjacent, and I could hear a tinkle of glass as she prepared some bottles. There was no crog loft in this cottage. Mam Meredith came back into the room, smiling and carrying her remedies. I thanked her.

It was such a beautiful day and so nice to be out of the nursery that I ambled my way home and, once through the village, sang my heart out to any listening skylarks or linnets. I sang all the folk songs I knew until I had exhausted my repertoire. Every time I tried to think of a new song to sing, the words *"If I've Jesus, Jesus only"* would come into my head. Quietly and tentatively, I hummed the melody. The words became clearer as I sang them out loud. Something stirred in my heart, like the feeling of getting out of bed and being excited about the day ahead. My heart woke up. I was revitalised and alive! I sang again, all the louder.

"When I soar to realms of Glory
And an entrance I await
If I whisper "Jesus only!"
Wide will open that pearly gate

When I join the heavenly chorus,
And the angel hosts I see,
Precious Jesus, "Jesus only,"
Will my theme of rapture be."

I came down into Nant and felt the heaviness descend on me again.

Non was in the nursery with her mam and William, when I took Mam Meredith's remedies up. She was quietly crying and Mrs Williams looked pale. William was standing by the window with his back to me, rocking Isaac. Non put her finger on her lips signalling to me not to speak. This domestic picture made me smile. I wanted to laugh so I put the salve and gripe water down and crept out of the room.

Later Mrs Williams came to the kitchen.

"Did Isaac settle?" I asked.

She looked exhausted.

"He stopped breathing, and went limp and blue," she said. "William was here. He picked Isaac up and immediately started praying for him."

I was shocked and felt bad that I had misread the situation.

"And?"

"Isaac started breathing again."

Chapter Seven

I crept out of the sleeping household without any sense of guilt and climbed to the farm. It was my day out, at last. Summer was warmly worming its way in behind spring. It always came surreptitiously, like a wild cat with its belly close to the ground stalking its prey. It was a foxglove year, and the purple plumes sprung up on the edges of the woods and tracks. The trees became laden in dark green, and the dog roses, honeysuckle and elderflowers perfumed the hedgerows. Mam Meredith's remedies and William's prayers had worked. Baby Isaac was getting fatter, but Non got thinner.

At the farm, I found the Gruffudds and William sitting around the kitchen table with the sun streaming in. They had just dipped the last sheep before the day warmed up and, with a tang of damp about them, were drinking tea and eating hunks of meat between enormous chunks of bread. I enjoyed their joviality and sat down to a mug of tea and a gammon sandwich.

"Go on, William, take Elin," said Uncle John as we finished and I saw him wink. I swung round to face William. He was laughing. They were contriving something.

"We're going to see the rocks in the valley, aren't we?"

"Oh, yes!" he grinned.

It was a warm, sleepy day, and we held hands and took our time as we climbed up to the valley. When we reached the *nant*, I splashed my face with cold water. A taste of salt touched my lips.

"*Tyrd*," William was saying. "Up here. I'll show you where the biggest deposits of gold have been found. Mr Ellis identified them." Mr Ellis—my heart missed a beat at the mention of his name.

William led me upstream, towards a big rock face. It was flanked by an enormous pile of scree that formed the head of the valley. Over the scree was the path to Trem y Mynydd. At the foot of the rock face there was a pile of wooden planks, a long iron jumper, some rope and a hammer. William stood over them.

"Are they yours?" I asked.

"No." He was perplexed. He ran his hand along the rock face and touched a hole, freshly drilled. With two fingers he explored the mouth of the hole and put his nose close to smell for gunpowder.

"I think someone is preparing to blast this rock," he said.

"Why?"

"I'm not sure, but the gold is up there," he said pointing above.

I could not work out where William was pointing. He laughed at me.

"Up there, Elin. Can't you see? There's that dark line of rock and just underneath it … there." He pointed.

I squinted and cupped my hand over my eyes to shade out the glare of the sun. I still couldn't see.

"Where?"

William shook his head.

"Look! I'll show you." He began to climb the rock face, stretching out his hands and feeling for a hold in the russet coloured rock. His feet edged their way across, reaching cautiously for a secure foot hold. His fingers and toes hooked and he hung against the vertical edge like a squirrel on a wall.

"Careful, William," I called. I didn't like it. The drop beneath him lengthened as he moved diagonally across.

"It's fine. I've done this lots of times."

All was silent and still, and I could hear the *nant* whispering further down the valley. The air was thick and heavy with heat. I shaded my eyes again and looked up at the ledge that William had now reached. Small, but big enough to bear his weight, he stood balanced and lithe, reaching across and calling down to me.

"See here, Elin?" He placed his palm flat in the centre of a line of dark rock.

"Here's the slate and here's some quartz. Do you see this rock here is a different colour?" He was pointing just beneath the darker rock. "There are lots of small deposits of gold in here." He stroked it affectionately.

"Aha! I see it!" I shouted.

William began climbing carefully down, feeling his way as he had done going up. Now in reverse, his eyes were on his feet. He went very steadily demonstrating his strength in each movement. So supple, he made it look easy.

I looked down towards the *nant*. A mine would bring a big change to the shape of this valley. I tried to picture it, opencast with sheds and wheels and wires. Like the quarry, there would need to be tracks and, perhaps, a railway.

Would a giant staircase be cut into Carreg Du, too? The valley itself would be unrecognisable. I wondered if the impact on our village really would be good. It might spoil it.

CRACK! My heart punched my rib cage as a sharp sound ricocheted around the valley and bounced across the rock face. What was that? My heart was thumping like pistons on a train. I looked up to see William spring back from the rock face as if he were stepping backwards expecting to land on solid ground and then, because there wasn't any, turn head over heels like a wheel on the winding gear, amid a flurry of small rocks. The moment froze his motion. No! This was not happening.

Silence! A rustle of small rocks fell like the last bits of sand an in hourglass. His boots peeped out from behind a big boulder. It was all I could see of him. I ran. Jumping and slipping over loose rocks, I stumbled and put out a hand on the dust to steady myself. Quick, quick! I skirted the boulder and there he was, lying in a foetal position, curled with his head beside the rock. There was blood on his hand.

For a moment, I stopped. Was he dead?

"William!" I called out. I was by his side and lifted his head. His face was disfigured with his eyes swollen purple.

"William!" I screamed at him. The panic rose. His cap had gone. I put his head in my lap and stroked his hair. I felt sick. He groaned a deep guttural groan. Relief washed over me with such force that I thought the contents of my stomach were going to be swept with it. He was alive! I breathed deeply to try to settle the nausea.

"William!" It was all I could say. He turned his head

slightly and a rush of blood fell onto my skirt. His ear was bleeding badly.

Help! I need help. Where could I get help? I scoured the valley. The *nant* ran down across barren ground and the ridge of rock we had climbed into the valley was empty. I turned the other way. There was a man. Another surge of shock pulsed through me. A man—was I seeing things? I wasn't sure. The sun was in my eyes and he was far away. With William's head still in my lap, I turned my body so that I could see more clearly and squinted against the sun. What a relief! What mercy! There was a tall man, in a trilby, silhouetted on top of the scree.

"Help!" I shouted and lifted one arm.

"Help!" I shouted again. My cry echoed around the valley and invaded the heavy silence of sleepy heat.

"elp— elp— elp." The sound bounced back to me.

The man turned and walked away, disappearing down the incline on the other side of the ridge out of sight. He had not heard or seen me. He must have! It was so quiet. It was so still. He must have seen me. How could he not?

"Help!" I yelled again at the silent surroundings.

William groaned and moved his legs. Oh! What to do? He might die any minute. Where could I get help? Should I run after that man? I stroked William's head again. He lay as a dead weight in my lap.

All of a sudden, I knew what to do. The quarry! It was closer than the village. I looked around for William's cap—something soft I could rest his head on. Then I ran, downhill like I had never run before, jumping the rocks and *nant*, out at the bottom of the valley, onto the path that led across the mountainside to the top of the quarry.

There were men there who could help, and stretchers.

When I reached the quarry and started calling, men began appearing like summer ants out of the cracks and crevices. They stared at me as if I were a wild animal and stood stock still. There was Ifan. He went white when he saw the blood on my skirt. He enlisted Gareth Thomas' Dad, who he worked with now, and a couple of other men as my story unfolded. Between them they carried a stretcher and came with me.

I was still feeling sick when we reached William. He lay as I had left him, his eyes bulging, and his head to one side on his cap, very pale and lifeless. Ifan knelt beside him and felt his pulse while the men discussed what to do. Somehow they made it all sound ordinary, like they were discussing a piece of rock. But they were tender. They gently tilted his body one way, then the next as they got the stretcher underneath him. The best way out was up the scree to Trem y Mynydd rather than down the valley to Nant, where the rocks and boulders would make carrying a stretcher difficult.

"Take him to Mam Meredith's," I suggested.

"Run on ahead, Elin. Tell her," Ifan said. "And then go for Dr Salusbury."

I scrabbled up the scree. The loose rocks slithered beneath my feet. When I reached the top I looked back down. The stretcher bearers looked small, far below. They were beginning a very cautious ascent. It would take them a while with four men, one on each corner.

Matthew, Mark, Luke and John,
Bless the bed that I lie on.

Four corners to my bed,
Four angels round my head;
One to watch and one to pray
And two to bear my soul away.

The odd little rhyme played over repeatedly in my head. I don't know where it came from, and in English too. It scared me. My thoughts began to form in prayer.

"Lord, please don't bear his soul away. Keep him alive. Help me find the doctor."

I heard a voice. I was at Mam Meredith's door.

"Elin, what is it?" She came and took my arm and led me into her cottage. I explained while waves of sickness and shock ebbed and flowed through my body, but her sympathy and concern kept me talking steadily. She made me drink some water and took charge. When she opened the door to her room and spread crisp white sheets out on the bed, I said, "I'll go for the doctor, now."

"Are you ready, *cariad?*"

I passed the men with William, coming up as I was going down. He still looked lifeless.

"William! William!" my heart screamed.

Dr Salusbury was in Nant with Mrs Hughes. He slipped his stethoscope in his bag, snapped the bag shut and set off. I went to get Mrs Williams and together we left the village, behind the doctor.

Chapter Eight

By the time Mrs Williams and I got there, Mam Meredith's cottage was made small and hushed, almost holy, with so many people in it. The doctor was in the bedroom with William and came out to speak to me. He wanted to know exactly what had happened. William was not making any sense. Telling the tale of the accident made it sound unreal. It had happened so quickly. Everyone listened and then the doctor spoke.

"From what I can see, William is suffering from concussion. His eyes are swollen and his head is bleeding but it is only grazes and bruising. It will heal. He may have some loss of memory and is unlikely to remember the accident. He may have some broken bones too, perhaps a few fractured ribs but until he can tell me where he is in pain, I won't know for sure. His hand is definitely broken. I have put a splint on it."

He asked Mam Meredith if William could stay where he was and not be moved again.

"Mrs Williams, will you stay with me and nurse him too?" she said.

I breathed in relief. Dr Salusbury seemed to think William was not in any great danger.

Ifan came with me back to the farm. He was reluctant to let me go alone, and when we got into the kitchen,

Mrs Gruffudd made us tea so sweet that again I thought I would be sick. I was exhausted from climbing in and out of the valley, over the hill and back. Uncle John, on hearing about William, tacked up Blodyn and set out to Mam Meredith's to see if he could do anything. Owen fetched Tanwen and she came and sat with me while I sobbed into my tea, the shock subsiding, before she walked me to the Manse. William had danced with death but Dr Salusbury had said he would heal.

The house was asleep in the sun. The gardener was dozing on a bench outside. I stumbled into the kitchen and disturbed Cook from her afternoon snooze. She took one look at me and exclaimed, "Whatever happened, *plentyn*?" She fingered my skirt where the stained blood had dried.

I glanced in distaste at the table, still covered with the remains of a meal, and could not think of food.

"Where's Non?"

"In her room," Cook answered looking bewildered. "Come, sit. Tell me, what's happened?" She pulled a chair towards the range. It scraped aggravatingly on the flags.

"In a minute," I said. "I need to speak to Non first. Her brother, William's had an accident."

My news woke the house into frightening activity. Non thrust Isaac into my arms and went to Mr Price's study. Within minutes they left together. I took Isaac to the kitchen. His mewing was irritating, and his wriggling unnerved me. I finally sat in the chair Cook had offered. She took Isaac off me, saying he didn't look safe, wrapped him tight and rocked him to sleep. She didn't press me for any more explanations. When Non came home I got up, washed my hands and face, changed my clothes and took

Isaac to her.

"How did it happen, Elin?" she whispered. "Mam said he hasn't spoken since she's been with him. He's just slept." I told her my unbelievable tale.

"How did he look?" I asked, and saw those purple swollen eyes, dark in his white face, lying beside the boulder.

"Horrendous. He's very pale and his face is all disfigured. His nose looks broken. Jabez has stayed." Was that to pray with him or offer him communion?

Later, before I went to bed I heard the quarry boom and guessed Ifan and his men had returned to work to make up for lost time, though it was late to be blasting. I was still awake, with the moonlight streaming in, when I heard Mr Price return and clatter up the stairs to bed. He'd been gone so long. Still, I could not sleep. I got up. I was thirsty. On the landing, I heard Non and Mr Price with their voices arguing, hers a hiss and his a growl. Non spoke with great vexation and her words were distinct and trenchant.

"Why would she want to kill him, Jabez? It was an accident."

I froze.

"She told me herself. He fell."

"William said she threw a rock at his head. He told me, *himself*."

He was angry.

"Mam said he would recover. She said he would be fine."

"He's lost a lot of blood."

I heard his footfall coming towards the door. It unbolted my nerves and I shot back up the attic stairs to my room before Mr Price found me eavesdropping.

What? What were they talking about? William wasn't dead, was he? Who threw a rock at his head? *She*? They weren't talking about me, were they? He wasn't dead. Panic and disbelief paralysed me. I stood in the beam of moonlight with my shadow elongated strangely on the eaves. It was not true. It couldn't be. The doctor said he would be fine, that William would heal. I shivered as the words "lost a lot of blood" echoed in my head.

There was no hope now. I couldn't sleep. My mind wouldn't settle and I crept between cold sheets and lay there numb. William wasn't dead, surely not. Was he? I would go to Mam Meredith's first thing in the morning. The more I thought the more awake I became. Eventually, to distract myself, I lit a candle, picked up William's Bible, opened it and read randomly where my eyes fell.

> *In the morning, LORD, you hear my voice;*
> *in the morning I lay my requests before you*
> *and wait expectantly.*
> *For you are not a God who is pleased with wickedness;*
> *with you, evil people are not welcome.*
> *The arrogant cannot stand*
> *in your presence.*
> *You hate all who do wrong;*
> *you destroy those who tell lies.*
>
> *(Psalm 5:3–6)*

I fell asleep then with the Bible open on my bed.

The summer sun rose early and, as soon as there was a hint of light on the horizon, I got up. Taking the gardener's bicycle from the potting shed, I set off out of the valley, but before I was through the woods, I regretted having brought it. It wobbled all over the place and the track was too steep for me to get any momentum going, so I resorted to pushing it up the hill. With some success, I managed to cycle the last bit of road before Mam Meredith's. I was praying with every turn of the wheel, "Lord, don't let William die. Make him well. Make him better. Repair every bone in his body. Mend his face."

I wheeled the bike against Mam Meredith's cottage and, peeping in, saw that she was up and busy, I tapped on the window and she came to the door, smiling.

"*Helo Elin*," she said in a hushed voice.

"I'm sorry I've come so early," I apologised. "I wanted to see William." Was he dead?

"Come in," she closed the door carefully, "and shh!" she warned. Mrs Williams was asleep in a chair. I followed Mam Meredith into the room William was in. He was lying on his back, very pale, his eyes still purple and his hands on his chest like a recumbent effigy on a tomb. The grazes on his face were clean. One hand was wrapped in bandages with a small piece of wood poking out beneath his fingers.

He was so still.

"Is he dead?" I whispered.

"No! He's asleep."

I didn't know what to do. I didn't want to disturb him, but I wanted to touch him and reassure him everything would be fine. My heart turned to prayer again and I stood there for as long as I could before I reached forward and put my hand over his good one.

"Make him better, please, Lord God," I prayed under my breath.

William opened his eyes and stared. His grasp tightened and recognition flooded his face.

"Elin." He said in a low and gruff voice.

Mam Meredith came forward quickly.

"*Bendigedig*. Your eyes are open."

"Huh?" He looked vacant.

"It's the first time you've opened them."

"Opened what?"

"Your eyes."

"Since when?" he asked.

"Since you fell, they were swollen shut with bruises and you couldn't open them," Mam Meredith explained.

"I fell?" The grip of William's hand got stronger. "Where am I?" He went to sit up, but on seeing his bandaged hand, put his good hand to his head and groaned.

"Oh, Elin, what's going on? Tell me." His discoloured, misshapen face gazed around the room with blood shot eyes. The bridge of his nose was swollen and grazed. Although some of the swelling had gone down, his eyes were still disfigured. He gave me a pitiful look.

I sat on the edge of the bed and took hold of his good hand again.

"You're in Mam Meredith's cottage. What do you remember?"

Mam Meredith left us.

"I don't know. What am I doing here?"

"You had an accident and you're here to get better. What do you remember from yesterday? We had a day out together."

"I remember dipping sheep, having breakfast and going for a walk up to the valley with you."

"Is that all?" I asked him.

"I remember walking with you, Elin. You washed your face in the stream and the day was very warm. I think I have been asleep. I had a dream that Non came and cried over me. I asked her what she was crying about. Then Mr Price, Gweinidog was standing over me telling me he wanted to kill me and that he threw a rock at my head. I woke up and found you here. Ow!" He put his good hand on his temple. "I can't frown," he laughed, "or laugh, ouch!" and he felt his cheeks. "Do I look a sight, Elin?"

"You do!" I was glad to see he hadn't lost his sense of humour. "Do you remember showing me the rock face?"

"No."

"You climbed it."

"Did I?"

"Yes, and fell off it."

"Did I?" he repeated. "Why did I climb it?"

"To show me where the gold deposits are. Do you not remember the holes in the rock and the tools that looked like someone was preparing to blast the rocks?"

"No. What was that?" William looked horrified.

"When we got to the rock face, there were some wooden boards and bits and pieces at the foot of it. You spotted holes drilled in the rock and said it looked as if someone was preparing to blast the face."

"Who would want to do that, Elin?"

"I don't know, William. When did you last see Mr Ellis?" He was watching me closely.

"The last time I saw Mr Ellis he said that they were trying to acquire a Take Note on the valley and to raise capital to build the mine. Owen has seen him more recently."

"Maybe they've got it and are starting work?"

"No. Owen said there's not enough capital yet. Only the Lloyds of Plas Horon have invested and Mr Price, Gweinidog. I believe he has invested too but, from the way he spoke, he seems to think it is his mine. I was so angry with his manner of speaking to me; I didn't listen well to what he was saying."

"I don't understand. He's friends with Mr Ellis," I told him.

"He is?" William's voice cracked.

"Yes, Mr Ellis was staying at the Manse the night Dad died. They were discussing geology together and talking about the river."

"Why didn't you tell me?"

"I was going to, but I got so muddled up over Dad's death and—" my voice trailed off.

Mrs Williams came in.

"William?"

"*Helo, Mam.*" He tried to smile. I let go of his hand.

"You look a lot better," she said.

"Elin has been telling me what happened, Mam."

"Yes, if it wasn't for Elin, William, you wouldn't be here," she said and fondly ruffled his hair.

"If it wasn't for me, he wouldn't have climbed the rock face." I felt bad.

"Your eyes are open." She ran her hand gently across his grazed face. "And you're talking sense, today. You said some funny things yesterday. How do you feel?"

"Everything hurts, Mam."

"Can you sit up?" She went to help him. I said to Mrs Williams it was time for me to go and when she mentioned the bicycle outside, I explained I had borrowed it. William laughed with immediate regret for the pain in his face.

"I'll come again when I can," I said. At least I had seen for myself that William was not dead. He was going to get better. God had answered my prayers.

I wobbled down the road through Trem y Mynydd and, on a whim, followed the track that circumnavigated Carreg Du. Laying the bike on its side at the top of the valley, I climbed down to see the line of gold and the rock face where William fell, again. Sliding on the scree, I scrambled down as fast as I could. I really should have been back at the Manse.

I didn't get very far. The valley, like William's face, was completely disfigured. The russet rock, where William had climbed was gone. Instead a new ragged escarpment of cracks and crevices were exposed. Rubble lay haphazardly where it had fallen. Crumpled piles of rocks were blocking the *nant* and the water had dammed up behind them. The whole rock face was shattered. I climbed back up to the bicycle, stunned by what I had seen.

I pedalled downhill with the pedals forcing my feet around rapidly as the land dropped away. I felt I would fly into my own accident if I didn't stop, so I got off, cursing the bike once again. I had planned for it to buy me more time but now regretted borrowing it, and even more so when the gardener shouted at me for taking it. He saw me put it back in the potting shed. I apologised and ran into the house without answering any of his questions. He moaned about me when he came in for his morning tea break.

Cook wasn't pleased to see me either.

"Where have you been?" she grouched. "We've got a guest coming today." I set to my daily chores, instinctively staying out of everyone's way.

Chapter Nine

There was shouting in the study. I stopped to listen. Isaac started crying. When I got to him, Non was there also in tears. She handed him to me and left without a word. Isaac worked himself into a frenzy before he fell asleep, exhausted. He expressed everything I wanted to, in his childish way. I would have loved to release my pent up frustration all in one tantrum. I laid him in his crib and returned to my broom. The angry voices fumed in the study.

Mr Ellis had come to stay again. He arrived in the heat of the day and, opening a leather wallet of papers, had immediately engaged in fiery discussion with Mr Price in the study. He had acquired a Take Note on Carreg Du, which meant mining could go ahead there. The intensity of their discussion warmed until it was fierce. Mr Ellis was angry with Mr Price, and there was no grace between them.

I stopped to listen.

"And just how do you suppose I am going to get Hugo Cranmer and Sons to come forward with the capital if they discover the rock face has been destroyed without the proper procedure?" Mr Ellis was livid. "This is all wrong! It's not how things should be done."

"It was the boy. He blew himself up in the process."

I nearly screamed. Mr Price was trying to say that William blasted the precious rock face. Why would he make a lie like that up? My blood began to boil. What game was he playing?

"The boy?"

"William Williams, the one you told me about, who showed you the deposits of gold. I told him to stay away and instead he drilled holes and blew it up."

"I don't understand. William Williams is sensible. He had good vision for a mine when he first showed me the valley. Could he have really done that, blown the rock up?"

Angry, I slammed the door in the hallway and the house shook. Mr Price, Gweinidog was a liar!

"What's got into you?" Cook asked. I couldn't trust myself, so I escaped into the courtyard and pushed the pump handle viciously until the water came spurting out. There was sweat tickling down my forehead when I stopped.

Mr Ellis needed to know the truth.

He and Mr Price went out together for the rest of the afternoon and came back just before dinner. Hot tempers had cooled and, after dinner, Mr Ellis retired early to his room with his papers, leaving Mr Price and his own brooding thoughts, sulking in a chair. Non had not joined them at the table. She ate in the kitchen with Cook and me, saying she was afraid of her husband. He was angry and irrational. She then went to her room, and I took her some tea. In a flash of inspiration, I decided to take a pot to Mr Ellis too. I knocked on his door.

"*Os gwelwch yn dda.*"

"Mr Ellis, a pot of tea, sir." I carried the tray in and

162

placed it awkwardly on top of a chest of drawers. My flash of inspiration had not inspired me with any idea of what to say about William. I stalled for time.

"Would you like me to pour it for you?"

"No, thank you. I'll pour it when I'm ready." He dismissed me.

"Sir," I said, "I'm sorry to interrupt you. I am a friend of William Williams."

Mr Ellis turned slowly and I noticed that his collar was not clean, nor were his cuffs.

"Your name is?"

"Elin, sir."

"William is an exceptional young man. What is it?"

"I wanted to tell you that I went with William, yesterday, up to the valley on Carreg Du. He wanted to show me the gold deposits he has shown you. He climbed up the rock face to point them out to me and then fell as he was climbing down. He was unconscious so I went to the quarry to get my brother who came with some other men and a stretcher. They carried him up to Trem y Mynydd."

"Where is he now?"

"He's still recovering in Trem y Mynydd."

"Does Mr Price know this?"

"Yes sir. He went to see William as soon as they heard about the accident."

Mr Ellis frowned.

"Mr Price told me William destroyed the rock face and himself in the process, but you are telling me he had an accident in the valley, yesterday, and fell." Mr Ellis thought for a minute. "Somehow the rock face has been destroyed but if William was with you and then incapacitated it means he could not possibly have blasted the place."

"No sir. William knows nothing about explosives. He's a shepherd."

"Oh, that's right. What do you know about rock?"

"Not a lot, sir, only what William has taught me."

"He is surprisingly astute. What was the rock face like then, yesterday?"

"Well sir, it was a normal rock face. As I said William climbed it."

"Was the stream in the valley blocked with blasted rock?"

"No sir. I think it was destroyed overnight. I thought I heard a blast at the quarry late yesterday, but maybe it wasn't the quarry, because when I looked at the rock face where William fell, this morning, it was in smithereens."

"Who did it then?" Mr Ellis asked. "Sorry, where did you say William is now?"

"In a cottage in Trem y Mynydd. His head is badly hurt." I described Mam Meredith's little home to him.

"Thank you, Elin. This is very interesting. Tell me, what did you do to your face?"

I fingered my scar, surprised he should notice it.

"I fell, sir, a few years ago," I said. "It was nothing like William's fall."

"It would appear that we all fall occasionally," Mr Ellis philosophised, with a smile.

The words "For all have sinned and fall short of the glory of God" came to mind. This Mr Ellis had an unusual way about him and I still did not understand how he fitted in with Mr Price and William both working with the same intention in the same valley. It might not have been right to speak to him.

"Lord, I'm sorry," I prayed in my heart. "I have done wrong."

The next morning, Non spoke to me. If I didn't understand Mr Ellis, I definitely did not understand Mr Price.

"Jabez told me that you made William fall. He said you threw a rock at his head. Did you?"

"Non," I answered in disbelief. "William is—do you really think I would do that?"

"No," said Non, "but I don't know what to believe anymore. I'm afraid of Jabez. I don't know what has happened to him. He keeps trying to tell me that you are a risk to us and insists you must go. He says you're a risk to Isaac."

Had she lost her mind? She sniffed, sucked her cheeks, held her breath and finally coughed.

"I am going to have to dismiss you, Elin. It's not my idea and not my choice, but it's either that or I have to defend you from his lies all the time. I can't persuade him otherwise. There is nothing I can do and, believe me, I've tried." Non began to cry. "You've got to go."

"You're giving me the sack, Non?"

"Yes," she said, and she handed me a package. "Here are your wages. Come I'll help you get your bag."

We went up to the attic and in tears Non helped me collect together my few belongings.

"Are you going to be all right, Non?" I didn't know where I would go, but wherever it was would be away from Mr Price and I was more worried about Non. His deceit was poisoning her mind and his words were binding her up in fear. There was no remnant of wisdom left in her.

"I've got Isaac," she said. He was no help, he couldn't protect her from manipulation.

Non picked up William's Bible.

"I recognise this," she said, and put it in my small trunk.

Cook was cross I was being dismissed.

"It doesn't make any sense," she said to the gardener drinking his tea.

"Hmm," he mumbled into his mug.

Non made me cry when I hugged her goodbye. It was all wrong and I was afraid for her.

Chapter Ten

Mam could not take me back home. Ifan's wage would not be enough for me too. I needed to find work. Swinging my trunk over my shoulder, with the handle behind my head, I balanced it on my back and set off for the farm. Uncle John was in the yard and saw me coming.

"Now this is the best thing that has happened today," he said, and took me into the kitchen. There was a great fire in the range and a big piece of meat turning slowly on a spit. It smelt delicious.

I told him everything: Mr Ellis, the rock face, Mr Price, Gweinidog, Non, everything.

"Well, *oen bach*, you can stay here. There's plenty to do. Or there's Llinos or Plas Horon, perhaps?"

The smell of cooking was enough to make me want to stay, and now that William was poorly, Uncle John must be in need of extra hands; only, Uncle John had sown a seed. Llinos! Poor lonely Llinos. She once said I was always welcome with her.

Uncle John spoke of William while a plan formed in my mind.

"He was looking a little better again this morning."

I finished the tea Uncle John had made me and thanked him. I left the farm for Mam Meredith's where I found William sitting up and he did look better. The grazes on his face were not so angry, and he was as colourful as the mountainside in spring with hues of red, blue, green, purple and yellow painting his face.

"Amazing what a good night of sleep can do." His smile, still a grimace and painful, changed the shape of his face.

"You were right about someone wanting to blast that rock face, William," I began, and told him how I had found rubble the morning after the accident. I told of Mr Price's lies and Mr Ellis' visit, too. William was disturbed.

"Mr Price, Gweinidog tells everyone a different story," I said. "And I don't know why, but I have these thoughts that haunt me." I explained them. "When you fell, William, there was a loud sound like a shot. Then when I shouted for help, I saw a man standing on top of the scree. He must have heard me. He did not come to help though. He turned around and walked away. The sun was in my eyes so I couldn't be sure but I think it was Mr Price. He's been telling Non I threw a rock at you, but maybe he threw a rock at you or even fired a shot? I don't know. Do you think it is too fantastic an idea?"

"He did tell me to stay away, to keep out of the valley and not to interfere with his plans," William remarked.

"I also think it was Mr Price who blew up the rock."

"Why would he do that? No, Elin. He doesn't know how to blast rock."

"It was all prepared for blasting with the holes drilled ready, remember. We saw it yesterday."

"I don't remember." William shook his head.

It was just an idea.

"I'm going to stay with Llinos for a while," I told

William.

"But what about your work?"

"Mr Price has sacked me. He has managed to frighten Non into believing that I caused your accident and am untrustworthy. I don't think she really thinks it but she's scared of him."

"Oh Elin! What a mess. I'm sorry. It sounds like Mr Price has gone mad. I'll have to come and see you when I'm better" and he squeezed my hand with his unbandaged one.

"It's all right. I'll be better off away from here. You'll need to stay away from Mr Price when you're well again."

I was just about to leave.

"Elin, have you still got my Bible?"

"Yes, do you want it back?" I picked up my trunk.

"No," he said. "I was just asking."

When I reached Llinos' cottage, she was exactly as she had been before and welcomed me in without question, like we were acting the same scene from a play.

"Can I stay with you Llinos?" I asked.

"Yes, Elin."

"Can I help you with your cockle collecting?"

"Yes, Elin."

Life was simple with Llinos. A daily pattern began to form. We slathered our legs with goose fat, hitched our skirts up high above our clogs and paddled in the shallows of the sometimes blue, sometimes grey, sometimes green waters. We raked through the sands of the flat estuary when the tide was out. A wind would whip between the island and

the mainland to taunt and sting us with its bitterness.
I realised then what a soldier Llinos was. She endured
isolation and ridicule but not only that: those sands were
cold, those waters ate you with a bite no goose fat could
protect you from, and yet she sang with her basket on her
head and carried on regardless. Misery was a word she had
forgotten when it came to work. This work was a balm to
her, and it became mine—out in the open air. Aware of
motion, shifting sand, water, waves at ebb and flow, there
was no constant, it kept you moving. The landscape kept
changing. I focussed on the moment, forgot how it had
been and did not worry about what would come, save to
keep an eye that I did not get myself trapped on a sand
bank.

We would come back with our catch and heat it up in
the cauldron, by her cottage. Then we would prepare the
cockles ready for selling and eating. The geese came to
nibble in the grasses, only pretending to take an interest
with one eye on us as we worked, waddling away in disgust
if we took no notice of them.

I became used to the rhythm of tides dictating our
livelihood, and occasionally we went cockling at night.
The tides never ceased. They just kept turning, sometimes
rising high and sometimes retreating far out to expose
a broad, flat bank of sand in the centre of the straits,
but always turning—a slap and splash on the shore, and
a ripple and rush far out. Llinos knew the cycles of the
moon well. Her life had been determined by them since
Jonny was alive.

As we set out one night, the stars winked and the
moon gazed between snatches of cloud that casually

drifted out to sea. There was freshness in the air, and when dawn began to hint at the horizon, it promised a warm day. I stopped and stood up, holding my basket on my head. Water dripped down my arm. I could see Carreg Du. Its silhouette, my familiar friend, looked so beautiful. The dawn light drew a line over its brow and along the profile of Trwyn Glas as it dropped into the sea. Then the sun rose like a gold cloak being lifted onto the mountain's shoulder. A handkerchief of cloud rested in the dip between the peaks. I felt pride at its well-dressed beauty—a possessive pride. The times I had enjoyed climbing that beauty, the rocks, the heather, the peaks, the valleys, were beyond counting. How much more of it had been blasted and sacrificed to the mine? I thought of William and the wounds on his face. How much of his beauty was lost? How was he recovering? He had said he would come and see me when he was better—soon, I hoped.

The following day, I discovered something that rattled my core and completely destroyed any peace in me. I was digging in the vegetable garden to enlarge a bed and make space for broad beans. There was an old pathway that had led to the cauldrons where the cockles and mussels were cleaned, but Llinos never used it now and it had grown over with weeds. I dug down deep, removing the dandelion roots and began turning up a number of bones. They were small, so I guessed Llinos must have thrown the carcasses of her geese here at one time, and perhaps her other waste from the kitchen. Each bone I put beside me and kept digging. I found a few tiny pieces of broken crockery. The soil was rich black. My trowel went deeper and deeper. I also found a piece of leather—a small leather pouch—a purse. Parting the lips that were drawn together by a thong, I looked inside. There were seven perfectly formed pearls. Pearls? Was I dreaming? I rolled them into my palm. They were cold and glistened. What a find! I stood up and took them to Llinos. She was behind the house heating water in the cauldron.

"*Edrychwch!*" I held the pearls in my palm out towards her. She looked at them, at me and then at the leather pouch in my other hand and shrieked. She ran past me and into the house, banging the door fiercely as she went. I followed her. Inside, she was leaning against the side of the fireplace sobbing. I put the pearls back in their pouch and went to her.

"Llinos. What is it?"

She ignored me. Her face was buried in her arms against the wall like a child. I could not make out what she was saying or sobbing so I put my hands on her shoulders, my ear against her back and as much of my arms around her as I could. She did not move.

"Oh Jonny." I made out from amongst her sobs. Then it sounded like she was calling "Sion". Her whole body juddered. My offered comfort was having no effect. I turned from her and fumbled for my pocket handkerchief to give to her instead. It was the one William gave me when Dad died. She took it.

"Sion, Sion," she moaned. Her words were clearer. Sion was her baby boy.

She turned from the wall and sat with her head in her folded arms at the table. I put the kettle on the range, sat back down opposite her and rolled the pearls out of the pouch onto the table. I fingered them. One, two, three, four, five, six, seven; they were lustrous, well-formed and worth a lot of money, I guessed. I put them onto the leather so that they would not roll off the table. The kettle was beginning to steam and I made some beef tea, thinking Llinos could do with it. She quietened while I was busy, and had pulled the pearls towards her, staring at them, vacant.

"Llinos." I went towards her again but she did not respond. I put a mug down beside her and still she did not move, so I sat down opposite her again and reached to touch one of her hands. She jumped and looked at me afraid. Had she forgotten I was there? She stared at me with the whites of her eyes wide and frightening.

"Llinos," I said sternly. "What is it?"

"Sion," she said.

"What about Sion?"

"They're his."

"These are Sion's pearls?" I asked, "Where from?"

"I gave them to him."

Sion was only a baby when he died. Why would Llinos give him pearls?

"You gave these pearls to Sion?" I looked at them again. They were perfect fresh water pearls. "Where did you get them from?" I asked.

"I found them."

"You found them?"

She nodded. "In the mussels," she said simply.

Did she collect them over the years of collecting mussels in the river? It took a long time for a pearl to form in a mussel's shell around a grain of sand that irritated the mussel. They were great treasure. Most people would sell them and make a nice bit of money.

"What do you mean you gave them to Sion?"

"I gave them to him, when I put him in the ground." Llinos said.

"In the ground?"

"Buried them in his grave," she said simply.

I thought of the little mounds of earth in the cemetery that Mam visited. Sion was not one of those. Where was his grave?

The whole story came into focus suddenly, and I felt sick. Those bones, I had dug up, were not the bones of geese. A feeling of nausea washed over me and I got up quickly and went back outside. The pile of bones was still sitting on the side of the little trench I had dug. I put them back into the hole and covered them over with soil.

Llinos was sitting in the same position, fingering the pearls gently on the table, when I went back in.

"How did Sion die?" I asked her.

"He got sick," she said without lifting her head. "No milk."

"Did *you* bury him?"

She nodded. My eyes blurred and I could feel the warmth of tears on my cheeks.

"Oh! Sion," I said. "Poor child, poor Llinos." Jonny died at sea and she was left nursing a baby all on her own unable to handle the grief. When her milk dried up there was no one to help guide her and teach her. Was it possible Sion got sick and died of neglect? Mam never told me the full story. Maybe Mam felt guilty too.

Llinos handed me the pearls.

"These are for you: for wisdom," she said.

"I don't want them." I tried every reason I could think of to give them back to her. "They're Sion's. They're worth a lot of money."

"You need wisdom," she said again and pressed them into my hand. "So have these."

I took them.

Chapter Eleven

There was a chill in the air that nibbled my nose, ears and fingertips. I barely noticed, just grateful to be outside. How often I had longed to work outside when I was cleaning the Manse. Today, I was weeding my new vegetable patch. I had made a little cross out of wood and put it on Sion's grave before I chose a new place to plant the broad beans. There was lots to be done.

The geese tried to help, dipping their beaks in the soil, dabbling about, and then slowly lifting their serpent necks to look at me with only one eye. Their pretence of looking always made me laugh. Silly old geese! They had come to accept me now that I fed them. I felt sorry that when the darker days of winter came, they would feed us. I would miss their hissing and honking. They were good guardians for Llinos' cottage.

The matriarch of the gaggle ruffled her feathers and the down on her neck stood up as, a little dishevelled, she waddled off beneath the apple tree. Three figures were ambling down from Moel Gras, beside the stream. I thought nothing of them and returned to the soil. It was surprising how much grew when the land was beginning to snuggle down to sleep for the winter. Autumn was drawing the shutters closed and, while there was still light, the stubborn weeds did their best to grow. We had agreed

I would stay with Llinos through the winter. She liked my company.

It was only when Madam Matriarch goose began to hiss that I sat back on my haunches and looked at the hill. Llinos came flying out of the door. It slammed behind her. She cried in delight to the figures walking towards the cottage, and I recognised the paisley shawl. Ceinwen had her arm looped through that of a man in a bowler hat, and there was another young man with them.

I went in to wash soil from my hands and found that Llinos had put the kettle on.

"*Croeso!*" she was calling from the gate, fussing the geese back out of the way. They flapped their wings and made a terrible din. I laid out some tea cups on the table. Voices mingled with the hissing of the geese and, as I was cutting and buttering a recently made *bara brith*, from the larder, the door opened. Rhodri Parry stepped in, removed his hat and grinned at me.

"*Helo, Elin!*"

"Hello Mr Parry," I replied.

"Rhodri, please! No *Mister* between friends," he said comfortably.

Llinos fussed with Ceinwen's shawl behind him.

"Ceinwen!" I was thrilled to see her.

"We brought someone else," she said. "We've just come from chapel."

She opened the door wider and there on the threshold stood William. I could have shouted so loud that all Caernarfon would have heard me. Instead, I bit my lip in surprise and grinned. He looked well. His grazes had healed completely, but I could see where they had been by the white lines they had left behind. I touched his cheek. Some scars were deep and ridged. He caught my hand and smiled.

"They'll disappear eventually," he said. "*Sut wyt ti?*"

"*Iawn diolch*. Come on in." I closed the door.

The kettle began to steam. Rhodri stood warming his hands. He watched Ceinwen. There was an understanding between him and her. I could see it, and when Rhodri and William were talking to Llinos about chapel, I asked Ceinwen quietly, "How come you are with Rhodri?"

Ceinwen smiled.

"But Rhodri is an engineer, Ceinwen," I said.

"I know, and in the kingdom of God there is no difference. The Bible says gentile or Jew, slave or freeman, we're all the same."

"I don't understand."

"Well, *cariad*, Jesus accepts and welcomes us, whoever we are and whatever we've done and, in his eyes, we're all equal. He helps all his followers to love one another with that same equality."

"So you're saying that you and Rhodri are equal in God's eyes?" I kept my voice as low as I could.

"I am! Rhodri treats me as his equal."

Mr Price, Gweinidog did not treat Non like that. What would Miss Evans, my old teacher, have thought if she knew how God saw men and women?

"He's been preaching all over the countryside and I have gone with him to help at the meetings," Ceinwen continued.

"Oh, did you walk together?" I joked.

"Of course," she smiled.

178

We talked and ate cake. The tea cups rattled in their saucers. The fire crackled in the range and we laughed like old friends. William had us in stitches describing the beautiful idiosyncrasies of some of the chapel folk. We might have sounded irreverent, but he showed no disrespect. Chapel came into most of our conversation. They said it was wonderful and that they had never seen anything like it. The Holy Spirit was changing people, and more people kept coming. No one wanted to miss what God was doing. They made it all sound so exciting, and a little frightening.

"I know!" Rhodri turned to me, "Why don't you and Llinos come with us to the evening service? I didn't think of it before, but we can walk back with you afterwards."

Llinos nodded to me.

"We'd love to."

"Come, then, we should set off very soon."

Ceinwen melted into the dusk-light by the door and returned with hats in her hands. Llinos lifted a hurricane lamp from a peg by the range and lit it. The dark was closing in and it was cold.

Once on our way, William hung back behind the others and took my hand.

"Mr Ellis came to see me," he said. "You were right, Elin, Mr Price did destroy the rock face."

"He did? Why?"

"He wants to build his own mine. He wants to do it all himself and only wanted Mr Ellis' advice and money, but he doesn't want anything to do with Hugo Cranmer and Sons. He's tried to get rid of Mr Ellis too."

"How?"

"He told Mr Lloyd lies about Mr Ellis and my accident, trying to make out Mr Ellis was to blame. But Mr Ellis took me to Plas Horon to speak to Mr Lloyd and they recognised that Mr Price was playing tricks. He has no morals! Mr Ellis said he was in a difficult position because of the money Mr Price had invested. But after I spoke with Mr Lloyd, he and Mr Ellis decided to form a new company and do without Mr Price. Mr Lloyd said he could find other investors, and he has asked Mr Ellis to be the director. Mr Ellis is going to break the agreement with Hugo Cranmer and Sons. Are you following this, Elin?"

"I think so."

"Mr Price has made the venture a mess and very difficult for everyone involved!"

By the time we reached Trem y Mynydd, I thought I understood. William spoke well of Mr Ellis and said Mr Ellis had been kind to him. If Mr Price and Mr Ellis had ever been good friends, as was the impression I first had of them, Mr Price had certainly lost the trust of a good man. He was a fool.

"Have you seen Non?" I asked.

"No. I can't go to the Manse!"

"I worry about her."

His hand tightened around mine. "Me too," he said.

I was hungry for the same nourishing experience I'd had when I had been to Mynydd Seion before. And that night, chapel did not disappoint me. I believed I could feel what Rhodri and Ceinwen had called "the moving of the Spirit." The Holy Spirit prompted people to stand up and sing, or pray or speak out. Just as the waters rushed back to join the waves of the sea in the pull of the tides, I felt drawn. I wanted to be completely immersed in what was going on, but I sat as an observer, not really knowing what to do.

It took me a long time to get to sleep that night. I first thought of William holding my hand as we walked to chapel and the scars on his face. I thought of Mr Ellis, Mr Price and the mine. I thought of Non, but what really kept me awake was thinking of baby Sion, Llinos' black-haired baby, whose grave I had disturbed. I felt uneasy that I had rearranged his resting place and that making him a cross hadn't meant anything. His little bones haunted me and a big, black empty abyss filled my mind. It terrified me. I froze, unable to move. What happens when we die? I was shivering. The question would not go away and nor would that terrifying abyss, with no beginning or end. I lay in the dark, paralysed by fear. With Sion I had found some pearls, some valuable treasure, but even thinking about those didn't bring me any peace.

I must have fallen asleep because I dreamt, as I so often dreamt, that I was climbing the mountains, but this time it was dark. There was a black mist all around me. I couldn't see where I was going. Suddenly a bright light, high up on the mountainside, started to come towards me. It swept up and down in rapid movement like someone leaping down the mountainside, carrying a lamp and covering the ground very quickly. Then I was in the light of the lamp and looking right into the eyes of a man. I shrank back.

"Elin," he said. "Come with me." I shrank back even more and turned away so that I could not see his eyes. They were as bright as the lamp itself. "Follow me. I'll lead you."

"Who are you?"

"Come. You don't need to be afraid." He held out his hand. "Look at this."

And I saw a great hole and hollow scar in his hand "I got this scar for you, because I love you."

In that moment, I knew who he was. I knew that the scar was where nails had been. I reached up and took his scarred hand. His grip was firm. I felt his strength and warmth spread up my arm and all across my body. My mind was filled with peace.

"You don't need to worry about death and dying if you come with me. Come, follow me. I died for you," he said, "so that you might be saved from dying."

Saved from dying, was that possible? Sion was not saved from dying, or Dad, or Gareth Thomas, or any of Mam's babies.

"Don't worry about them," he said as if he had heard my thoughts. "There is more to life than life in this world. Come with me and you will live."

Peace surrounded me. I knew that this was Jesus, himself, speaking to me. Looking at those eyes and feeling that firm, comforting grasp of my hand made anything feel possible. I wasn't even sure if I was dreaming or if I really was out on the mountainside. I just knew I believed every word he said.

I awoke sweating, and the moon was shining in on my bed. It had been a dream, but there was a presence in my room. He was there.

"Jesus," I spoke into the air. "I want to come with you." I looked at my hand. It did not look any different but it was tingling from his touch. I held it out as I had done in my dream. "I want to come with you. I want to follow you and live this life with you," I said again. There was a whisper of wind and my heart felt full and still. He said he could save me from dying. I believed it.

"Thank you."

The moonlight was very bright. I could see an arc of water droplets had gathered in the corner of the window pane. I lay there for a while and heard the words of my recitation ring in my mind.

Y rhai a breswyliant yn y tywyllwch a chysgod angau, yn rhwym mewn cystudd a haiarn:

Some sat in darkness, in utter darkness,
prisoners suffering in iron chains.

(Psalm 107:10)

Dug hwynt allan o dywyllwch a chysgod angau; a drylliodd eu rhwymau hwynt:

He brought them out of darkness, the utter darkness,
and broke away their chains.

(Psalm 107:14)

There in the dark it came to me. The light! In my dream, Jesus carried a light. The Psalm said he brought them out of darkness and broke the things that bound them. He set them free. Every death that had touched my life had frightened me and shrouded me, even Sion's. I wanted to be out of darkness and free. Free, with no need to fear death. Free, with no need to fear *fear* and now I felt much lighter, like chains of anxiety had been taken away from weighing me down. He had brought me out of darkness and into the light.

I thought of Non.

"Jesus, please go and speak to Non, just like you did to me. She needs to see you. She needs to be free from fear too." Hers was a different sort of fear. She had every right to fear her foolish husband, but if only she could be free from that fear.

Ynfydion, oblegid eu camweddau, ac o herwydd eu hanwireddau, a gystuddir.

Some became fools through their rebellious ways and suffered affliction because of their iniquities.
(Psalm 107:17)

Mr Price had become a fool for gold.

A cloud passed in front of the moon and it all went dark. I brushed my hand across my scar. I felt foolish. What right had I to talk to Jesus? William had called himself a sinner and now I understood why. In the light of Jesus, I felt ashamed, inadequate and imperfect. I could criticise Mr Price as much as I liked but I was no different.

"Forgive me, too, please Jesus!" I said, like I remembered William calling out in chapel. I remembered the scarred hand of Jesus taking hold of mine in my dream and I was filled with calm so steadying it was like an anchor had been tied to my soul and thrown to the bottom of the ocean. It held me firm and secure while the waves of doubt tried to rock me to and fro. He said he had acquired that scar because he loved me. All my faults and failings were in that hole in his hand and instead he filled me with strength, hope and acceptance when I held his hand.

Assured, I fell asleep. When morning came, he was still there. I had slept in peace and, when I woke, I reached for William's Bible. It was dark but dawn was not far off. I picked up the Bible and it fell open. I went to stand by the window where a glimmer of light was beginning to show from the horizon and began reading,

> *The whole earth is filled with awe at your wonders;*
> *where morning dawns, where evening fades,*
> *you call forth songs of joy.*
>
> *(Psalm 65:8)*

I saw again the unfolding of a cloak of gold over the brow of Carreg Du and Trwyn Glas as on the dawn when Llinos and I were up cockling. That was God's wonder, His morning chorus, His song of joy.

"Sing," Jesus was saying to me. "Sing with me as the sun rises". He was there. An excitement fizzed in my heart. With all that peace inside me and the joy I felt, I began to sing, not so loud as to disturb Llinos, but just enough for him to hear me. I closed my eyes and sang the only song from chapel that had stayed in my head.

> *"What though clouds are hovering o'er me,*
> *And I seem to walk alone,*
> *Longing, 'mid my cares and crosses,*

185

For the joys that now have flown—
If I've Jesus, "Jesus only,"
Then my sky will have a gem;
He's the sun of brightest splendour,
And the star of Bethlehem.

What though all my earthly journey
Brings me naught but weary hours,
And in grasping for life's roses,
Thorns I find instead of flowers—
If I've Jesus, "Jesus only,"
I'll possess a cluster rare;
He's the "Lily of the Valley,"
And the "Rose of Sharon" fair"

I opened my eyes and glimpsed that the shroud of mist on top of Moel Gras was beginning to lift. I sang on, with soft tones growing, a crescendo.

"When I soar to realms of Glory
And an entrance I await,
If I whisper, "Jesus only!"
Wide will open that pearly gate;
When I join the heavenly chorus,
And the angel hosts I see,
Precious Jesus, "Jesus only,"
Will my theme of rapture be."

I meant every word I sang. My body vibrated with a resonance that rushed through me. I knew his presence. He was my dawn, my light, there with me. So this was what William had meant when he said that you need to see Jesus to understand. This was what Ceinwen meant when she said she had met Jesus in the chapel. This was what Mared meant when she said she was redeemed by her Saviour. I knew I had seen him and now I could see him with inside eyes. I knew he was there. I could speak to him with an unspoken voice and he heard me. I could see his hand in the lifting mist and majesty of Moel Gras. He knew I could see. It was overwhelming.

Chapter Twelve

The door swung wide behind me and Llinos padded in. I turned. She looked lost.

"Llinos?"

"Elin?" She looked at me quizzically. *"Oeddech chi'n canu?"*

"I was singing!" I stepped forward to embrace her. She looked cold. With her head cocked to one side, she stepped back as I got closer.

"It is a pretty air—" she said hesitantly and turned and padded from the room. Dear Llinos!

"It is a pretty air," I agreed. More than an air to me, it was an anthem, a declaration, a disclosure of the most precious treasure I have ever found. I was loved and accepted.

"Llinos," I called after her, but she was gone.

The following Sunday she came with me to chapel. I could not wait to go and stood with William's Bible under my arm, while she fussed with her hat and pins. She kept changing the angle of it on her head—this way, then that—until I impatiently told her it would do and pulled her outside. The frosty grass crunched under our feet. We reached the chapel before the doors were open, and sat outside in the sun, watching our breath make little clouds. There was a bitter breeze coming up from the sea.

It wasn't long before people started drifting in with cheerful calls of "*Bore da*!" Ceinwen came with the crowd from Plas Horon and was surprised to see us sitting there. Llinos went into chapel with her while I waited for William. I was looking forward to seeing him.

He came on his own and was just tucking his cap in his pocket when he saw me.

"Elin!" he exclaimed.

"William, I wanted to talk to you." I said. He caught my excitement.

"What is it?"

I told him my dream. I told him I had seen Jesus. I told him I now understood what he and Ceinwen had meant. I said I could feel Jesus here with me, even now, and that it was the most amazing thing. I told him how Jesus had said "Follow me," how he had told me he had died for me and how he had promised more than life in this world, in living life with him.

There, in front of all the people coming into chapel, William put his arms round me and swung me with whoop of exuberance until my feet left the ground.

"I'm so glad," he laughed as he put me down. I felt ten foot tall.

We went into chapel and I sang like I have never sung before. Every word I prayed, I meant, and I knew that Jesus heard me. Every other word spoken felt like it was him speaking to me. He was there. I listened. I felt the Spirit move. I knew I belonged.

Llinos and I went to chapel every week. Llinos transformed like a butterfly emerging, growing more confident around people and she began to care about her appearance. Her titivating before we left became more than being about her hat. Her shawl was folded and rearranged several times and her skirt shuffled around and brushed. She'd put her face up to the mirror and pull the creases around her eyes up and down. Eventually she would decide she was ready. There was a spark in her step and fire in her eyes. Her language began to change and her conversation became peppered with the phrase "God willing." I heard her recite the Lord's Prayer every night before she went to sleep, until she was asking everyone she met if they "knew Him".

We killed three of the geese over the winter, providing plenty of meat and fat and lots of fresh feathers for our pillows. I slept so well. Sion's pearls still lay in their leather pouch beside my bed and disturbed me occasionally. Llinos had given them to me 'for wisdom' as she said, but I needed a good dose of wisdom to know what to do with them. They were valuable. If I sold them, the money should go in Llinos' pocket, but I knew she didn't want that. I was uncomfortable about keeping them and equally unsure about selling them. Then I had an idea. It repeated itself over and over in my mind and I knew it was the right thing to do. I had to act on it.

One Sunday morning, as spring began to bud again and my seventeenth birthday had passed without anyone noticing, I picked up the pearls, in their leather pouch, and took them with William's Bible to chapel. When the bags were handed around for people to put their money in, I slipped the pearls in hoping no one would notice. I hoped Llinos hadn't seen. I wanted to give them to Jesus. I handed them over to him. As I did so, I heard him say in the quietness of my heart, "This is what you need to do when anything worries you—cast your cares on me."

The quarry, in Nant, was at a stop while repairs were being done on the jetty in the quay. A scaffold had been built that only a few of the men could work on. So while no granite could be shipped, the quarry had stopped. There was news too of a visiting preacher, well known by many. He was coming midweek while the men were out of work. Even the newspaper publicised his visit. Llinos and I decided we would go and listen to him.

It was a brown sort of day when we set off with the wind tussling our skirts and shawls. We took the track between Carreg Du and Trwyn Glas, and when we reached the streets of Trem y Mynydd, we found a throng of people already six rows strong outside the chapel. We waited awhile, greeted our neighbours and discussed the weather. I recognised Ceinwen's friend, Huw Piws. He smiled at me and nodded, touching his cap. I smiled and nodded back, remembering the small encouragement he had given me when Gareth had died in the quarry accident.

I found William and stood by him.

"I've got something to show you later," he said as he greeted me with a kiss on the cheek.

The door of the chapel opened and a number of men emerged. Uncle John was with them, looking very serious and his beard very pronounced amongst the younger men. A man I didn't recognise spoke earnestly with him and the minister. They were observing the crowd. It was huge and still growing. The stranger stood on the top step, facing outwards, preparing himself to speak. His forehead was furrowed and his face honest. The crowd around us hushed in anticipation. This was the great man of God everyone had been talking about. The Spirit of God was with him and wherever he went refreshing came.

He opened his Bible and spoke clearly and authoritatively, slowly enunciating each syllable in the musical rise and fall of the soft valleys accent.

"If my people, who are called by my name, will humble themselves and pray and seek my face and turn from their wicked ways, then I will hear from heaven, and I will forgive their sin and heal their land." (2 Chronicles 7:14)

He read and we waited, breathless, to hear what he would say.

"When you come to listen to God and not a man, I will preach."

He stepped down into the crowd and was lost to sight.

That was it! That was all he was going to say?

The crowd remained hushed. He had rebuked every single one of us. This life with Christ was not about "us". It was not about great men. It was not about glorifying what God had made. Our lives were to bring him glory, make him known just as his creation around us did. In a very simple way, the preacher had turned every one of us back to God. You could see it in our faces. People began to pray. They went down on their knees.

"Forgive us, Lord," was the united cry.

I closed my eyes and saw Jesus' face again, just as it had been in my dream. His eyes were bright and they reassured me. I was filled with love for him and began to hum.

"If I've Jesus, "Jesus only,"
Then my sky will have a gem."

Voices around me joined in until a swell of voices
sung in unison. That same thrill of joy washed through
me. With our faces upturned we sang, and rain began to
fall. The great chorus harmonised and hymn after hymn
was sung with the sense that Jesus heard, cared for and
cleansed his people. His work on the cross was complete
and evident among us and so we sang:

"Mi dafla' 'maich oddi ar fy ngwar
Wrth deimlo dwyfol loes;
Wrth deimlo dwyfol loes
Euogrwydd fel mynyddoedd byd
Euogrwydd fel mynyddoedd byd
Dry'n ganu wrth dy groes."

Through the falling rain and crowd of people I saw a
slim figure with her head down at the edge of the crowd.
Hope leaped inside me and politely, I elbowed my way
towards her.

"Mae'n ddrwg gen i," I kept apologising. As I got closer
to her a small boy swung round her skirt. I knew it. It was
Non. I called and she turned. She kissed me.

"Elin, I am so pleased to see you."

"And I, you! How are you?" But before she could
answer I crouched down and tickled little Isaac under
the chin. *"Helo, dyn bach."* He stared at me and did not
respond. In my eagerness to know everything I asked,

"How is Mr Price, Gweinidog?"

"He left me," Non said simply.

"No."

"Yes. And the village, because of the mine. He was angry with me and everyone who got in his way. That mine!" There was a hint of bitterness in her voice. "He said it was his idea, it was his project, it was his company, it was going to make him money and make him well known." She shook her head. "It was going to make the village thank him and respect him for bringing innovation and new life to the village, he said. It was all about him, Elin, and how it would benefit him, not how it would benefit anyone else. Oh! You know what he could be like. You saw him. He and Mr Ellis had many rows. I was afraid for Mr Ellis and I went to Mam's. I didn't like being in the house when Jabez was angry. And then he just left. I didn't know what to do. I went back to the Manse, but I heard nothing from him for weeks until some men came and told me he had resigned his position. They said I would have to leave the Manse. I asked for an address for him, but they had none. So I took Isaac to Mam's and have been living with her since. William suggested I come here today. It's very different, isn't it?"

"Yes, you can see God at work here. I've been praying for you, Non."

She hugged me like a sister.

"Life without Jabez is so much easier in some ways and harder in others. I'm not sorry I haven't heard from him, but it's strange not knowing where he is. It's strange for Isaac's sake. I'm living like a widow, but out there somewhere is a proud, self-centred, angry man," she said. "You were better off when you left us too, I'm sure. William told me you were living with Llinos, and when I heard that, I didn't feel so bad about dismissing you when I did. It turned out all right for you, didn't it?"

It did, more than she could have known.

I stayed with Non while the singing continued so that she wouldn't be left standing on her own at the edge of the crowd. The rain eased off and people began to drift away. They were damp, but refreshed. I guessed Llinos would be with Ceinwen but before I could find her Uncle John found me.

"Come to the farmhouse. We're all going back there to warm up and dry out. And you too, Non. Hello little fella," he said, picking up Isaac. "What a fine young man you're becoming."

William was amongst those heading down to the farmhouse, too. He caught up with me by the track around Carreg Du.

"Elin," he called. I stopped and turned. With his cap in his hand and his hair glistening with rain drops, he looked different.

"Did you see Non?" I asked.

"Yes. Isn't it good to see her and Isaac? Come, I've got something to show you," and he signalled to Uncle John, who nodded. "Come with me." He took my hand and led me onto a freshly made track alongside the one we had been following. Recent use by many carts had made muddy furrows. Though the track was new, we weren't far along it before I pulled back. It looked different, but I recognised where we were going.

"I don't think I want to—" I said hesitating. I hadn't

been back since the day after the accident.

"It's all right," he reassured me.

"But—"

"I promise you."

I shook my head. In a flash I saw his face, swollen purple, as it had been when he'd fallen. "I can't." William stopped and turned to me.

"You must!" He put an arm around my waist. I felt his muscle flex across my back, and gently he guided me. For a minute, I studied him. His face had changed. It took me a moment before I realised how.

"Stop! William look!" I put my hand on his cheek, "Your face, it's different." No more white lines. No more small raised ridges of flesh. "Your scars have gone."

He ran a hand down his cheek himself while staring at me and then laughed. He reached out and touched my eyebrow.

"Yours has disappeared too," he said in wonder.

Chapter Thirteen

Our scars had gone. Without apprehension, but with awe, we walked forward into the valley of gold. It was a miracle. Our scars had disappeared and it made us feel bold and special. While we had been singing and praying, God had done something impossible. He had reversed the irreversible and removed the marks of the past. I remembered Jesus' scar, his hand.

The valley itself had completely transformed with buildings, and scaffolding, paths and tracks, and it had been carved much wider by the blasting of rock. I was astonished. This must be what William wanted to show me. Gone was the hurrying *nant*, heading for the trees. It was tamed and dammed into a wide pond and channelled out through neatly constructed leats. One led to a water wheel.

We stood at the edge of the pool. Our clean reflections smiled back at us from the still water. William's head was bare and the wind ruffled his comedy of curls. My hat was lopsided.

"We're so human," I said, sounding foolish. "We make mistakes and yet God can turn the mess we make into something good." I shifted William's Bible, which I had carried from the meeting, into the other hand and stepped closer as I tried to say what I meant, but William wasn't listening. There was an agitated energy contained in the hunch of his shoulders and deep thrust of fists in his pockets. His freshly shaven chin jutted towards the mill.

"They built that with the rock Mr Price blasted," he said.

"Is there gold in it, then?" I joked.

"No," he smiled and pointed. "There might be fool's gold, but the real gold deposits are up there where I fell." He was being very serious, all of a sudden.

There was nothing in the landscape that I recognised except the colour of the rock. I shuddered. The image of William's face was in my mind again. I turned to look at the miraculous change in him. His skin was so fresh, as if he had just washed in the *nant*.

"I wouldn't be here if it wasn't for you, Elin," he said.

"Oh dear, don't start." I still blamed myself for making him climb.

He took his hands out of his pockets and faced me.

"But there's some truth in it."

"No there isn't," I frowned and looked down.

His fingers whispered across my cheek and lifted my chin. The gentleness of his touch made me hold my breath. I had not noticed the pattern of blue quilling, like roses painted on porcelain, around the dark pupil of his eyes before.

"May I?"

I waited. He shook his head and answered, "No, not yet."

I breathed again.

"Come. I have more to show you." He took my hand and though he had held it many times before, today felt different. I was conscious of how perfectly my hand fitted

198

into his, like a jigsaw puzzle piece, made to measure.

"What if you had died, William? I couldn't imagine life without you," I said. "You've always been my closest friend." His hand tightened around mine and I saw the scabs of grazes on his knuckles.

"What have you been doing?" I asked.

It was true that William had been my closest friend, for as long as I could remember. He was a man now, so amiable and winsome. What did the future hold for him? I was different, too, now. Could I follow him as I had always done on whatever adventure took his fancy? The reality pressed down on me. No! No more adventures; there was life to live and work to be done. We'd grown up. He would go his way shepherding the sheep with Uncle John and I would go mine, helping Llinos collect cockles on the coastline far away from the valley. She had also become another person, so sure of herself. Her shame had gone with her fear of strangers and she shone with an innocent joy. The revival in the chapel had changed her and others perception of her. Did she still need me? I needed her— that was certain. I needed her for a livelihood. What else would I do if I didn't live and go cockling with her?

William had once said he had Jesus to guide him. I remembered, and Jesus had said to me that when anything worried me I should give it to him, like the pearls.

"Whatever my future holds, please guide me and be with me, Jesus," I prayed in my heart.

We stepped over planks and around piles of stone, walking through half built buildings. There was wood, mud and rock everywhere.

"This is where I work now," William said very simply. I

thought I'd misheard him.

"Why didn't you tell me?"

"I wanted to keep it as a surprise. Come, I'll show you where." He led me down to the lower end of the valley. It had been opened out wide with a short row of buildings built looking out to sea. The old path I had followed to reach the quarry, on that fateful day, was still there and ran behind new buildings. William led me to the door in the furthest building from the head of the valley. He pushed it open. Inside was a tidily furnished room with a table and chairs by the window, a rocking chair by the range and mirror on the chimney breast. It looked as if someone lived here.

"This is where you work?" I enquired, incredulous. It looked like a home not an office. It was delightful.

William laughed. "No," he said, "I'm teasing you, Elin." He was his jaunty self again. "This is where I live."

"Where you live?"

"Yes. I have been given this cottage by Mr Ellis and Mr Lloyd's company. It's mine, rent free for as long as I work for them."

Open mouthed, I turned to face him. "Rent free? How can that be?"

"They gave it to me, they said, as a thank you for showing them the gold deposits. This valley is rich and the gold here is especially rare, but they have also found copper and tin. They wanted to honour me."

"That's wonderful, William. What work do you do?"

"I'm an apprentice." He grinned. "I've helped build everything in this valley."

"It's perfect, so perfect," I exclaimed. He wasn't always

going to be a shepherd. "Your dreams! They've come true. You said they would if you put Jesus first in your life."

"Only eighteen years, and I dream of much more," he said.

I put his Bible down on the mantelpiece. It fitted exactly the width of the mantel. There was a jug of elderflowers and dog roses beside it. They must have been freshly picked because neither last long, out of the wild.

"I can't believe this is your home. I'm glad." My gasps of surprise continued to fill the room as I looked around. "So did you build this cottage, too?"

He nodded.

"Yes. I helped. I have learnt a lot." He rubbed the grazes on his knuckles.

"Look at that view!" There was the sea and Nant. No! Nant was hidden beneath the mountainside. It was tucked away. Only heather, bracken and blue water were visible. I stood savouring it, taking it all in, the beauty of my favourite mountain. This was its prettiest side.

I noticed a grey stone wall by the cut of the valley. It was the wall of the cemetery where Dad now lay.

> *Where, O death, is your victory? Where, O death, is your sting?*
>
> *(1 Corinthians 15:55)*

The words resonated in my memory as something Mr Price had read at Dad's funeral but strangely I knew it was Jesus reminding me that he was there.

William, with his back to the door, was watching me in the light of the window.

201

"Elin," his voice was hesitant.

I looked at him. He was uptight, again.

"There was one thing we forgot to put in this cottage, when we built it," he said.

"Oh? What was that?" I stepped up to the rocking chair and casually putting my hand on the back, looked around the little room again. It was cheerful and light. Somehow the sea reflected into the room and made it brighter. A petal from one of the dog roses had fallen onto the black metal of the range. The pink and white heart-shape was the only thing out of place.

William came up behind me. He slipped his arms under mine and faced us both to the mirror pulling me to him in front of the fireplace. We stood there looking, framed, his cheek resting against mine. Our reflections smiled back at us, again; my hat still tilted and his curls unruly. The anxiety in his face dissolved as I melted into him. I could feel his warmth and solidity firmly supporting me and he smelt of the fresh outdoors.

"They forgot, to put a wife in this cottage," he laughed, "a wife without spot or blemish," and he gently stroked my healed eyebrow.

"Will you? Will you be that for me? Be my wife."

Felly dyweded gwaredigion yr Arglwydd, y rhai a waredodd efe o law y gelyn

Let the redeemed of the Lord tell their story
(Psalm 107:2)

Glossary

Words

Afon .... *River*

Arglwydd .... *Lord*

Baban .... *Baby*

Bach .... *Little*

Bara Brith .... *A Welsh tea bread*

Bendigedig .... *Fantastic*

Caban .... *Cabin—*
where the quarrymen would gather to eat and talk.

Caniad Solomon .... *Song of Solomon*

Cariad .... *Love*

Caseg .... *Mare*

Cinio .... *Dinner*

Croeso .... *Welcome*

Cwtsh .... *Hug*

Diolch .... *Thank you*

Edrychwch! .... *Look!*

Ffynnon .... *Fountain*

Gweinidog .... *Minister*

Gweddi .... Prayer

Helo .... Hello

Llongyfarchiadau .... Congratulations

Lobsgóws .... A Welsh stew

Mawr .... Large

Mynwent .... Cemetery

Morwyn .... Maid

Na .... No

Naddo .... No

Nain .... Grandmother

Nant .... Stream

Oen .... Lamb

Peswch .... Cough

Plentyn .... Child

Putain .... Prostitute

Piws .... Purple

Sêt Fawr .... Large Seat—where the elders and deacons traditionally sat at the front of the chapel.

Storom fawr .... Great storm

Tatws .... Potato

Tyrd .... Come

Ynys Môn .... Isle of Anglesey

Y Parchedig.. The Reverend

Wfft! .... *interjection—So!*

Phrases

Ble mae...? .... *Where is...?*

Bore da .... *Good morning*

Da iawn .... *Very Good*

Dwi'n mynd .... *I'm going*

Dwi wedi fy synnu .... *I am surprised*

Dydy o ddim yr amser .... *It's not time*

Dyn bach .... *Little man*

Fy mab .... *My Son*

Ga i dy helpu? .... *Can I help you?*

"Gwyn y gwel y fran ei chyw er fod ei liw yn olau ddu" .. .. *Welsh Proverb: "The crow sees her chick as white even though it is black"; meaning every mother sees her child as beautiful*

"Huna blentyn, nid oes yma ddim i roddi iti fraw" .... *Welsh Nursery Rhyme: "Sleep child, there is nothing here to frighten you".*

Mae ddrwg da fi .... *I am sorry*

Mae ef yn gyda chi .... *He is with you*

Mae'n ddrwg gen i .... *I'm sorry*

Mor fawr â hyn .... *This big*

Oeddech chi'n canu? .... *Were you singing?*

Oen bach .... *Little lamb*

Os gwelwch yn dda .... *Please*

Sut wyt ti? .... *How are you?*

Yma heddiw .... *Here today*

References

Biblical quotations are taken from the NIV Bible
(English) and Y Bibl (Welsh).
Words to hymn "*What though clouds are hovering o'er me*"
by Hattie M. Conrey
Words to hymn "*Mi dafla' 'maich oddi ar fy ngwar*" by
William Williams Pantycelyn

Postscript

Before I came to Wales my concept of the country was fuelled by the poetry of Gillian Clarke and Dylan Thomas, pictures from an AA book of walks and the description a school teacher from Wales gave. She described a country full of remote beauty, mountains, sheep and chapels. None of this prepared me for the kindness of the people, the stunning landscape or the rich heritage; all of which stir my imagination. I fell in love with the place and it has now become the country I have lived in longest. Its charm has not worn off yet.

I wanted to write something that could express the love and respect I have for the place and its people. I wanted to write something that might capture some of its heritage and perhaps make the reader want to visit, see the landscape for themselves and mix with amazing people. Whilst the story of Elin and William is fiction it is permeated with real facts and inspired by true stories.

Throughout its history, Wales has managed to maintain a unique and vital expression of faith somewhere within its borders and has bred men and women that have inspired others and carried this faith far beyond its borders. Christianity has never died out in Wales, even when Britain experienced the dark ages, and has always had a stirring religious culture. The dates 1859 and

1904 are particularly significant years in Welsh history, during which thousands converted to Christianity. It was unprecedented and dramatic. Local communities and culture changed as a result. These are known as 'Revivals'.

Elin's Air is set in the years around the 1904 Revival. Much of Wales was affected and the transformation that took place in lives and communities made national headlines. There are many unique stories from around this time and *Elin's Air* captures a flavour of the sort of things that took place. The lyrics of the hymn, important to Elin, are sung to the tune of '*Dim Ond Iesu*'. This tune we recognise today as more familiarly set to the words '*Here is Love*'—a hymn associated with the 1904 revival. Some of *Elin's Air* bears a close resemblance to actual stories. One I heard told was that when the revivalist, Evan Roberts came to preach at a chapel in the Nantlle Valley, a great crowd turned out to see him. He refused to preach on account of the people who came to see him, like a celebrity, rather than to meet with God. This story is referred to in *Elin's Air* but Evan Roberts is not named. The only real minister to be mentioned by name in the book is Rev. Job, from Bethesda. His faith and leadership played a significant role in the Bethesda chapels at this time.

The strikes (known as 'the Penrhyn lockout') described in the lives of Elin's family, at the Penrhyn quarries in Bethesda really did happen and were painful. Between 1900 and 1903 the community struggled, due to labour disputes with Lord Penrhyn. It is still cited as an unprecedented industrial dispute. There are people, today, who will not visit Lord Penrhyn's gothic castle (now a

National Trust property, near Bangor) as a matter of principle because of the distress caused to their ancestors. The quarries were never as successful after the lockout and the area is still scarred with signs of industrial decline.

The newspaper report, from 1903, of Lloyd George speaking at a chapel opening in Bangor is a genuine article. His concern for the decline in chapel attendance was articulated prior to any significant change taking place and gives us a feel for the religious climate before the full impact of revival in North Wales was recorded. He also gives great esteem to preaching and its important place in Welsh culture at the time. Lloyd George was born and grew up in North Wales and went on to become the British Prime Minister during World War One. As a Liberal politician growing up in a part of working-class Wales, he was instrumental in helping structure the social welfare we are familiar with in British culture today.

Reference to Edward VII's coronation and the work of Mr Lister in saving his life are also true. His coronation, in 1902, was postponed at short notice due to illness and Mr Lister performed surgery.

Some places referred to are real, Bangor, Caernarfon and Barmouth for example, but the actual setting is fictitious and loosely based on the granite quarries of the Lleyn Peninsula. Gold has not been specifically mined on the Lleyn, though Welsh gold has been extracted since Roman times. There are ruins of gold mines to explore in Coed-y-Brenin, near Blaenau Ffestiniog and the remains of other small and successful ventures in the Dolgellau area. Since 1923, the British Royal Family have been wearing wedding rings fashioned from a single nugget of

Clogau gold extracted from the Clogau St. David's Gold Mine, near Barmouth.

The mining company and characters in *Elin's Air* are all fictitious but some inspiration came from an open cast mine on Anglesey, now no longer worked. Parys Mountain was famous for its diverse mineral extraction and was a very productive mine. One fortunate employee was given a cottage rent free, for life, when he discovered gold.

Cockle and mussel harvesting, also a traditionally Welsh industry, was more prevalent in South Wales and along the Pembrokeshire coastline than the North. However, the Conwy estuary and Dee estuary have had their share of cockle and mussel harvesters over the years. In Wales, it was common for women and families to work at collecting cockles, to wash them in heated cauldrons and sell them in local markets. Cockles and laverbread, made from seaweed, formed part of their staple diet.

Anyone familiar with Welsh religious culture might recognise the description of the picture '*Salem*' by Sydney Curnow Vosper. To save this painting from becoming an anachronism in *Elin's Air* I changed its name to '*Gweddi*', meaning 'prayer'. Painted in 1908, '*Salem*,' depicts the interior of a chapel in North Wales. It now hangs in the Lady Lever Art Gallery of Port Sunlight, near Liverpool, but has become an iconic image of Welsh chapel life from the Edwardian period.

Some might feel that the development of the relationship between William and Elin, to the point of him asking her to marry him, rather rapid or that they are too young. The attitude towards marriage and the pattern of responsibility and maturity was different. It was expected that youngsters would marry earlier and with a simpler courtship than today.

I have purposefully created the feel of a more Victorian way of life in the community described, though *Elin's Air* is set in the very early Edwardian era. I have done this because rural Wales has a habit of hanging a few decades behind the rest of Britain when it comes to progress and change. The pace of life is more relaxed.

Come and see for yourself!

About the Author

Emily Stanford lives in North Wales with her four ponies, three dogs, two cats, chickens and sheep. She also has a humorous husband and four fantastic children. Writing is her solace and excuse to escape from everyday busyness and the landscape and heritage of Wales provides ample inspiration for things to write about.

https://emilystanford.org/

Lightning Source UK Ltd.
Milton Keynes UK
UKOW05f0249060417
298474UK00006B/87/P